WHERE I FALL
WHERE SHE RISES

We gratefully acknowledge the support of the Canada Council for the Arts and the Ontario Arts Council for our publishing program. We also acknowledge the financial support of the Government of Canada.

Where I Fall, Where She Rises is a work of fiction. All the characters and situations portrayed in this book are fictitious and any resemblance to persons living or dead is purely coincidental.

Cover design: Val Fullard

Library and Archives Canada Cataloguing in Publication

Title: Where I fall, where she rises : a novel / Dean Serravalle.
Names: Serravalle, Dean, 1973– author.
Series: Inanna poetry & fiction series.
Description: Series statement: Inanna poetry & fiction series
Identifiers: Canadiana (print) 20190094087 | Canadiana (ebook) 20190094095 | ISBN 9781771336253 (softcover) | ISBN 9781771336260 (epub) | ISBN 9781771336277 (Kindle) | ISBN 9781771336284 (pdf)
Classification: LCC PS8587.E7748 W54 2019 | DDC C813/.6—dc23

Printed and bound in Canada

MIX
Paper from
responsible sources
FSC® C004071

Inanna Publications and Education Inc.
210 Founders College, York University
4700 Keele Street, Toronto, Ontario, Canada M3J 1P3
Telephone: (416) 736-5356 Fax: (416) 736-5765
Email: inanna.publications@inanna.ca   Website: www.inanna.ca

WHERE I FALL
WHERE SHE RISES

A NOVEL

DEAN SERRAVALLE

inanna poetry & fiction series

INANNA PUBLICATIONS AND EDUCATION INC.
TORONTO, CANADA

ALSO BY DEAN SERRAVALLE

Chameleon (Days)
Lock 7
Reliving Charley

For Alaia,
the light of my life

CHAPTER 1: LEA

A POEM KEPT ME ALIVE to write my story. I can't believe I have simplified it to this reason, but it's true. A poem I studied in an English Romantics class in university saved me from torture, death, war, and myself. It also introduced me to my greatest love and my greatest fear. "The Marriage of Heaven and Hell" by William Blake. Who would have thought it could change me in the end?

Everyone else in my second-year class hated the poem, except for Paul. I hated *him*, how beautifully contrary, because I love him now.

He parted his hair to the right side, and I prejudged him American proud. This I remember with vinegar on my gossipy tongue. He was so unnatural, unlike me, who let my hair curl out, like weeds. This I remember with embarrassment and regret. I never thought I would attend university in another country. However, when I earned a scholarship to Columbia in New York City, I had to go. I needed to separate myself from my mother. She wanted me to enter the town convent. After my father's funeral, our parish priest told her he had dreamed of me. I had become one of the statues in his church.

I told her I wanted to find stories to tell instead. My mother hid in other rooms and prayed behind my back to keep me pure. I suppose that's how you save someone's soul when she's not looking to do it herself.

Before officially putting this story to paper, I scratched her out in many beginnings. I didn't want to start with her or him: the journalist I had always envied, and the fanatic mother I blamed for everything wrong in my life. I suppose I was never good at beginnings, or first impressions, for that matter. I could never look someone straight in the eye. If anything, I turned people away from me by glancing elsewhere in a conversation. This is a talent I mastered after my father died. I earned a doctorate in it after my marriage failed.

You see, I lived an entire life believing an Old Testament God was punishing me. That this same God took his vengeance out on me and me alone because I ignored his phone calls. In my small town of Thorold, the priest called it not heeding "The Call." I simply heard a voice in my ear. When I finally achieved freedom, I studied alongside Paul and we graduated in the same year. Never friends, really. Just passersby with the same ambitions. We applied to Globe News Network internships right after graduation and we were hired on the same day. Overnight, Paul became famous. I got married, moved back home, practically died from an overdose of small-town normal, and found myself in purgatory after the U.S. Iraq invasion of 2003. I did freelance reporting in the red zone of Baghdad. Every day, I wished for someone to kill me other than myself. Because I couldn't. Because I just couldn't.

So this is where my story really starts or interrupts. In Baghdad. In the red room.

BY MY OWN CHOICE, I slept alone in the red room. I occupied it after the invasion of Baghdad. It was all red: red velvet wallpaper, red shag rug. Before the invasion, a citizen might have called it a hotel room or a brothel. After it was abandoned, it became my shelter and a place I might have called home if not for the way I existed there—without notice. In order to hide my solitary residence in the hotel, I kept the room dark. It turned blood-red some nights. Pictures of young men with scarves covering their mouths hung in my bathroom in the glow of a red heat lamp. Other portraits floated in the tub, developing, enlarging, never sinking. Some of my photographed subjects held semi-automatic weapons across their shoulders. They posed proud like actors in a black-and- white documentary film.

On the night Paul got a hold of me, I poked at the pictures in the tub with a pencil to keep them wet. Foreign voices rose into the red room on a trail of cigarette smoke. A pack of hoods had stopped to meet in conversation at the foot of the deserted building. I had grown accustomed to the speed of their language. At times, I was able to pick out repeated words, like *enemy* or *blessed*. During the day, men with similar purpose sought shade in the gaping hole there. A misfired rocket bomb had carved it out. The whole complex shook from the inside out when it struck, nearly collapsing inward on me.

I pulled my legs to my chest and crouched into myself, wishing them away. Adnan was bound to arrive, and I didn't want to be found. I wasn't supposed to be alive. Another dead reporter once told me I would never survive alone in the red zone. And yet, there I was, breathing. Actually, that night, after a clicking noise sent a gun off I was hyperventilating. The noise triggered some laughter outside the building. I cupped my ears with my hands and tried not to imagine the worst; that they shot someone for the sake of testing a new toy. The gun fired again and again until the laughter stopped and a silence replaced it. From the blindness of my bathroom, I couldn't determine if they had walked away or simply eliminated themselves, one by one, the last with a choice to live alone or die with his brothers. I could smell gun smoke seeping in through the broken window—much more powdery than cigarette smoke. I considered relocating. It wasn't safe staying in the same place for too long. But there was running water in this building.

On my knees, I made my way to the boarded-up window. The voices had evaporated and disappeared into the night leaving only the sour scent of sweating skin behind. When I needed to move around in the red room at night, I crawled to avoid casting shadows. By hand, I felt mould in the shards of rug and scratchy, hard spots. When I touched these spots, I imagined a woman made to feel like a servant here, or a prostitute, or maybe, the victim of an unsolved murder. I palmed around for the wet spot, a spill from the previous night. After finding it, I pressed my face on its dampness. Its scent was still sharp, and I wanted to lick the spot before it dried with the morning air. Before the odour of engine oil and melted rubber invaded the room with clouds of dust and sulfur. I rubbed my face in its dampness like a cat recognizing its territory. If I needed to, I could suck it dry and spit the shards of carpet in a corner like a ball of fur.

I had faith in Adnan. Adnan was bound to arrive soon.

I watched the door.

And then my laptop beeped with a message.

I edged closer to it, beneath the broken window covered in newsprint and alongside my bed, where I kept my belongings, all except for my camera. Well, Joel's camera when he was alive and working with me, taking pictures. I had wrapped it in a dirty towel and placed it in the trash can. He would have approved of the hiding spot.

When I reached the laptop, it cut out. Attached to a satellite transmitter with a rubber antenna, the screen stuttered until I shook it alive. While I waited for the message to reappear, I tried to peel the label of an empty bottle nearby. The glue was hard though, and my hands were shaky.

The screen finally whitened. Paul Shell had sent me a message from the green zone. It read,

Lea,
As I sit restless in this green room, I am remembering our college days at Columbia. Back then we had sharp teeth for stories. We were searching for our own Vietnam, a war of contradictions to

enable our passions. Do you recall those early times as fondly as I do? Staging rallies without a real cause until the planes struck our city with brimstone and fire. We saw the opportunity and sacrificed our lives to stage our voices. Together, we sold our souls to GNN and our beliefs to television. And then, in the Registan desert, I broke the story of a century. Do you remember?

He was always bragging even when he thought he was telling another story.

Red sand stung my eyes and burned my face as I stood like an explorer of explosions in the distance, my head above the gun turret. I was a war prophet to the world then. Fire rose from the sand and the smoke made night before my eyes. Until a stray bullet found a bone in me forcing me home. A famous bullet that locked me in a studio room with a camera. I think I died for the first time when I saw my clean reflection in the lens. I was porcelain to the world, smiling with false white teeth before commercial breaks. I was preserved with wax and paint and pinned against a paper backdrop. Now that I'm in Baghdad, I'm not interested in pretty stories with empty shells.

I was lying nude on my belly, facing the laptop. St. Jude on a rusted medallion tickled the keyboard from my chain. Also Joel's. I was ready to write something to Paul. The man with the face a country trusted. The man with the musical words to help you fall asleep at night, even after witnessing a crying woman in a foreign land pulling her hair out over a bloodied child. The man who was always giving you his resume or slipping in his journalistic accomplishments to remind you of the absence of yours (which would never really compare anyways, according to him). Your prototypical, egotistical, celebrity journalist, who always needed praise to justify his own view of himself. I typed a response with my two forefingers.

Paul,
I do remember those days. We were equals then, in school. In the same classes, at the same parties, never close enough to really like each other, even when we were hired by GNN in the same hour.

I recall how envious I was of you for going over first, for being selected to leave everything behind. It was the day I hated my marriage most, playing house against my will, each day watching my life grow stale in packed lunches and evening sitcoms with laugh tracks. I would stay up late at night to see where you were in the desert, to hear your voice claim stories I desired to claim.

And then it happened, and my envy found you. I was watching that day. It was the day you became the news you were reporting. The day the world pitied you for receiving a bullet that didn't kill you. That day inspired me to leave everything behind to find my own stories in another desert. I understand how it must have hurt you to come back home.

Perhaps you should have died that day, although I think I can save you now. I have what you are looking for, but I need to see you in person. It is a fragment of a story. I will give you what is left of it before it drifts away. Meet me at The Argument.

When I hit "send" an explosion shook the building. I didn't flinch; it was far enough not to cast a light in the room. Improvised explosive devices often sounded to me like church bells in the distance. Never at the same time. Always to signal the release of a lost soul. I glanced at the screen, spotted with my fingerprints, expecting an immediate answer from Paul.

Instead, there was a knock at the door. I crawled over on old scabs to answer it. A *niqab* that hung on the wall from a leftover nail brushed my face like a curtain. I turned the lock and opened the door without thinking of danger. Adnan was crouched low, anticipating me as he would a pet awaiting scraps. His face was wrapped in a grey scarf, but his eyes smirked beneath a line of dark eyebrows. He was too young.

This I knew without ever seeing his face. In his oily hands, he held my desire in a paper bag.

I crawled backwards to let Adnan in, hoping he would accept his regular payment, praying he wouldn't mind if I cried again while he took it. I sat up, splayed my legs, and leaned back a little to tease him. I forced a smile, which if not sexual, was certainly submissive, and that was all the same to him. The cold St. Jude medallion slid to my back. He finally handed me the bottle, closing the door behind him. Without removing his boots for the carpet, he unbuckled his pants, except I don't remember hearing the jingle or the zipper of his designer jeans.

As he prepared himself, I took the bottle to my chest and cradled it like I would my own child. My legs widened further as I ripped the seal on the bottle. At the request of my raised hand, he stopped himself from removing his scarf. His weight pressed me down on my back eventually. He was polite enough to lean to the side so I could drink at the same time. I heard a *beep* signifying a response from the computer screen even before he released himself into me. I didn't wait for the jingle of his belt tightening before leaning over and reading the message through the blurriness of the empty bottle. The glass stretched the words, making them appear like they were written longhand instead of typed.

"I will meet you at The Argument, *'for [this] man has closed himself up, till he sees all things thro' narrow chinks of his cavern'*"

I knew the poem Paul quoted well. We had studied it together in school. I would see him soon in the red zone.

"WHAT ARE YOU STILL DOING HERE?" I asked in a firm tone. Adnan sat on my bed watching me dress as if studying my body for another story to tell. The way his shoulders slumped made him appear like a boy in trouble, awaiting admonishment from his teacher. If not for the scarf covering his face, I may have felt the need to call his mother.

"Watching you," he answered.

"I have to get ready."

I was purposely rude, but he wasn't getting the hint. I rolled up the *niqab* against my chest into a black tire, pushed my head through the hole and let it slide over my shoulders. It stopped at my bony hips. I had to tug on it to cover my legs.

"Where are you going?" Adnan asked, his English accent getting better.

"To meet someone."

"For drinks?"

"For conversation."

"You need more drink, Lea."

"You don't know what I need."

I understood his aspiration to act like an adult in control of his actions, how he craved to show maturity after the brief sexual interlude. But he was still a boy. Yes, he could get me alcohol and ride his little Vespa motorcycle at top speed against passing traffic, but his experiences were too limited to justify the loaded gun he carried with him or these feeble attempts to prove he was worthy of being respected as an adult. He stared at the empty bottle, the one with its label intact. I had refused to offer him any. I was almost sure he had never had a real drink, although he had seen others experiment. Like most street soldiers his age, he devoted himself to a cause where justification of one hypocritical act like murder required the adherence to other religious principles, like abstinence from vices, although sex with me had managed to slip through the cracks of both. I continued to adjust the *niqab* so that it hung looser on my body, so that it wouldn't appear like a disguise.

"What are 'chinks'?" he asked. He had turned his attention to reading the computer screen now. I walked over to the laptop and slammed it shut, offering another hint for him to leave. The glow of the dawn from the window projected the newsprint characters on the red wall now, black and inverted and with a boozy distortion from the screen. I must have aged a century in the light to him. The sight of me with my short hair flattened against my head must have tainted his dreams of a future wife.

"Where is my picture?" he asked.

"Not ready yet."

"Where is it?" This time his voice cracked, as a spoiled child's would after not getting his way.

"In the tub, but don't touch it."

He walked into the bathroom, and I watched him in the reflection of the cracked mirror above the chipped armoire in the room. He knelt down before the tub and eventually found his reflection, floating with others of his generation. I had taken a new picture of him recently because he thought the previous one didn't identify him properly. In this retake, he held his father's rifle across his chest, pointed to the sky. I could see him in the bathroom smiling on his knees, approving. In black and white, he must have appeared more real to himself, historic. In this particular photo, I had captured him in a soldier's pose, ready for battle and old enough to survive it.

He stood up to recognize some of his friends hanging on a clothesline above the tub. Although they were members of different sects and insurgent groups, they acknowledged a brotherhood in uniform. How unfortunate, I had always thought, that they needed a war to justify family bonds and the principles of sacrifice, honour, and courage often fed to them by their storytelling parents and grandparents. I tried my best to capture all of them as men, but in their frozen eyes, I could always detect the fear of boys. After he lifted the toilet seat, I felt embarrassed when my book slipped from the ledge behind it. It was small, thick, and leather-bound. Religious. I could hear the syringe that marked the page escape and roll about the floor. I had used an elastic band to encase it tightly, holding the old binding and improvised bookmark together.

"Don't flush the toilet," I called out, remembering I had to get ready in order to escape the building unnoticed, hail a cab, and meet Paul on time at The Argument.

"It will overflow," I shouted again in an attempt to encourage him to come out. I didn't like him alone in my bathroom. My personals hung to dry on the clothesline as well, some with stains I couldn't brush away without soap.

It got silent, and then I could hear him urinating in the toilet that held mine, an orange stain lining the inside of it. Once again, the impossibility of keeping up the room in this abandoned hotel embarrassed me.

In the reflection of the mirror, he reached for the knot at the back of his neck. He was preparing to remove his scarf in order to wash his face and hands at the same time. With no desire to see his unobstructed face, I looked away as he undressed. I didn't want to see how young he really was or how innocent he might have been before the war, before meeting me after Joel was shot, before helping my real photographer to an area in the shade so he could die there in the cool.

I scavenged the damp carpet under the bed to find the information I would offer to Paul. In my peripheral vision, Adnan exited the bathroom, and I knew he had walked out of it with a naked face. He was trying to prove something to me, but I wasn't ready or prepared for such a confrontation. I pretended to be searching for more things under the bed.

I assumed he had more important errands to run for someone else, which would profit him more than spending time with me. These insurgents always had errands to run. I resolved to wait for him to cover his face with the scarf before I turned around.

"Where do you want this?" he asked.

His voice had changed to a muffled, deeper tone, and I was relieved he had reapplied the scarf. He held my book, the one that had fallen in the bathroom.

"Just set it on the chair," I pointed.

He gravitated closer to me with soft steps, feigning an air of penitence. When I finally looked up, an expectant look widened his eyes, questions lingering in-between them. He wanted to show me his face. He had come to trust me enough to reveal it. Most of all, he pillaged for more, perhaps a conversation, or someone to confess a crime to. Maybe he just wanted a friend he could share his doubts with, like how he felt about the death of one of his brothers in the throes of guerrilla warfare. Or maybe he needed to ask me questions about myself. He must have wondered what kept me in Baghdad, taking photographs of rebels, drowning myself in the dry desert air with alcohol and heroin. He must have assumed I would have left after my photographer died. Or at the very least, moved to the green zone, where journalists were protected. He might have even wondered what I searched for in the red zone, and why I punished myself in the process. He had probably known strong women in his life, like his mother or an aunt who had lost her husband to the war, who now tended to a large family on her own. And yet, he was still not mature enough to help me in return.

"Thank you," I said, again hinting it was time to leave, for the both of us. He nodded to obey, not to understand. He raised his hand to the scarf again, as if about to take it off. He had that insecure look in his eyes, like I would find him ugly and wish him to leave and never come back. I pitied him and wanted to reassure him that his face would only be one more ghost to haunt me in a moment of regret or guilt. And I was harbouring one too many already.

I folded the sheets of paper from under the bed into small squares to stuff into my shoes. A rush of adrenaline strengthened my pliant legs, so much so, that when I rose to my feet, he flinched back.

"When will it be ready?" His voice had deepened.

"When I hang it up and it dries," I answered.

"They will be disappointed and will hold payment."

"If they want the picture, they will have to wait. You can't change time or the air."

He walked by me and left the red room without a goodbye.

That same sour, sweating scent of his skin disappeared when a panzer tank rumbled by the abandoned hotel, sending sand into the room. For some reason, I felt like I had killed another opportunity to listen, and be good again, if only for a minute.

THE EGGSHELL-COLOURED CAB drove me through gassy mirages rising from the asphalt. For the first time, I noticed the loneliness of the city's palm trees. They lined the burning streets, one every couple of miles or so, each making no shade on its own. It was a vampire desert. Space and sand and planetary air. My driver was sharp-chinned and glossy, like one of my pictures floating in the tub. The desert brightness made him wear darker glasses. Every once and a while, I saw his grey eyes in the rear-view mirror. The scratchy radio cackled with a string of stirring speech followed by a speeding lute, while graffiti stains blurred by as we accelerated beyond plastered buildings. Other guerillas had posted my pictures alongside their messages. I suppose I made many of them famous, while they rewarded me with food, drugs, and stories in return.

A blockade of honking cars congested traffic up ahead, but the driver was not prepared to stop. He would crash if the blockade didn't move. The cab's meter flipped red numbers like a stopwatch and as he shifted the gear, the shaft dropped making a broken sound. I braced myself before he swung into another lane, hurtling over the meridian.

Everyone was in a hurry for the war, or rather, afraid to stop in the midst of it. Furious motion was the best way to avoid perishing by coincidence. Or maybe it was just smarter to be a moving target.

A convoy from another world boasting English words on its storage cab nearly side-swiped the car. It picked up speed as an airplane would on the runway. The cab driver made a sharp turn in the opposite direction. Children kicking a can scurried away like insects seeking a hole. In this small enclave, I finally saw the basement café. No sign, only a lamp in the window and the common knowledge that it was called The Argument, or a place to discuss, with hostility, opinions over drinks.

A soldier opened my door and paid the fare. Like the desert on the way in, he was dressed in sand- and-white spotted camouflage. With his rifle, he pointed to the stairwell leading down. A military jeep blocked the entrance.

I lifted the *niqab* to step down the stairs. I noticed in the light that my feet were as white as the stone steps. I craved another drink.

Paul sat at a table away from the lamp in the window. I could see him in the hospitable darkness. A clear drink waited before my empty seat like a mediating friend.

"Thank you," I said, nodding to the drink as if it understood.

"I thought you might need one."

"I'm not so thirsty anymore."

I took it anyway and finished it in one cyclical motion.

"It's very risky meeting you like this," he leaned in to whisper.

"The story will make up for it in the end," I explained in a mocking tone of voice.

A woman's hand extended from a black sleeve to place another clear drink before me. She must have heard the empty jingle of unmelted ice in the glass. Coincidentally, the waitress was wearing the same black *niqab*, but as a uniform rather than a disguise. I wanted to wait or show manners by not drinking it in one swig again, but it didn't matter here, as it didn't matter anywhere in the red zone.

"Is it credible?" Paul was trying to attract my attention, shift it away from the fresh drink before me.

When his face struck the light from the entranceway, I saw him on television again with his designer glasses and short, preppy hair parted to the side. He was clean-shaven, ready to break stories. I hadn't plucked my eyebrows in years.

"Why wouldn't it be?"

The sound of an impatient foot, tapping under the table, moved me to remove the folded paper from my flat shoe. It was damp from my foot, while his hands were soft when I pressed it into his palm. Although he couldn't read in the dark, he unravelled it and placed it close to his eye. I could see his Roman nose pressing into it.

"We'll air it tonight," he affirmed.

"With your voice?"

"Yes, with *only* my voice."

Although I should have been insulted by his unwillingness to source the story or involve me in its delivery, I cared less and less about the credit. In the red zone, I had learned that survival alone was motivation to stay alive, that story was shallow without some suffering in its discovery, even if it was self-inflicted suffering. The story would die a little more with his voice, and yet, it was more valuable in his possession.

"Do you miss your life in New York?" I asked.

"Do you miss your life in Toronto?" he asked in retaliation.

"No."

"My wife is in New York," he said.

"With child?" I had heard rumours.

"With my unborn child."

I found enough etiquette in lapsed time to down the second drink. As if attached to another by a string, a full glass stretched its way from the floating black *niqab*.

"Don't you want to return for the birth?" I asked. I didn't want to remember my own birthing experience with this question, but I couldn't help myself.

"You know, '*The just man must keep his course along the vale of death. Roses are planted where thorns grow.*'"

He smirked as if to imply I would have forgotten "The Marriage of Heaven and Hell," the one poem we studied together for an entire semester at school, before I returned home to Canada.

"Yes, but, 'On the barren heath sing the honey bees,'" I replied. I didn't want him to think he was so smart.

He was more relieved I remembered it.

"If only life was the memory of a poem." I sought the left-over alcohol sheathing the ice at the bottom of the glass with my tongue.

Then, the tables shook, and smoke came in to fill the room.

CHAPTER 2: **CAROL**

THIS MEMOIR IS MY SECOND BOOK, not to brag. This version of myself should be truer than the first. A pathetic ghostwriter handled that one. Although, it did make me famous enough to get this opportunity. My agent thinks this story will save my relevance. The other made me a celebrity, but celebrity must be nurtured and destroyed for it to keep everyone's attention. At least, that's what Timothy says. He looks after me in so many ways. Every version of me, that is.

So, in my first memoir, the story revolved around what happened to my husband and how I dealt with it. How his story victimized me, and how I defeated it in the end. This memoir needs to come from my perspective, this time around. And I need to confess. Confessions are raw, and people like raw, or so said my agent. Especially since my first version made me a statue of perfection. The all-American wife of a kidnapped journalist on the other side of the world, eight months pregnant. Not a bad premise, no? Bestseller, baby!

What everyone doesn't seem to know is how it really happened on my end. Not the fictionalized version, the non-fictionalized version, with all of its ugliness and "rawness."

According to Timothy, my fifteen minutes of fame will expire if I can't shock the world into paying attention again. I know he will always love me since he created me. Once you get a taste of the world feeling the same way, it's hard to let go. I suggested a number of ideas, but what happened between us seemed like the scandalous way to go. Saints were once sinners, weren't they? Isn't that the formula? That you could fall, get up, and shine like you did when you were innocent?

With that said, I believe it is time to tell the real-life story behind the creation of Carol Shell, celebrity wife, mother, and widow. A woman desperate to be loved anew by the world. But who isn't, now that I think about it.

IN THE TIME BEFORE I FOUND OUT about Paul, I refused to watch television until nine o'clock in the evening as a way to protect my unborn child from the violence of the world. Nine o'clock was when Paul's face would appear on the screen, and it was his voice I wanted my baby to hear, and his voice alone. Most of the prenatal books I read pointed to the importance of hearing voices from the womb. It's where family bonds began and instinctive connections were wired. And I didn't want my baby to be born with the sensibility of an adopted child—always seeking for the ghost of parents past. My books recommended other little tricks. I had all of them strewn about the coffee table. Yoga for pregnant women. The organic recipe bible advising which fatty acids were essential and which I could ignore. Stories to read to your child before birth. I took my herbal tea in the living room, which is where I liked to read. Reading passed the time more fluently than waiting to see if Paul would reappear on the television screen.

Although I detested it before I was pregnant, I allowed classical music to filter the silence of our urban condominium. Beethoven's *Emperor Concerto* trickling through the surround sound speakers hidden in the walls. I had read about the IQ benefits and purchased the audio set from the Disney Company. I had read everything twice to make sure, always aloud for my unborn baby, even though I hated the echo of my own voice in the condominium. An echo that pervaded since Paul didn't like carpets. As he often reminded me when I sought a place we could both call our own, it had been his condo before we were married, and it held sentimental value. Or maybe it was just a museum for his past conquests.

The baby kicked hard at the sound of the phone, so I often left it unplugged. When a knock sounded on the door that day, the baby nearly kicked through me.

"What are you doing here?"

I was surprised to see Timothy Abel at my door without my husband by his side. He was dressed in a three-piece, pinstriped suit, with a red tie, stars falling below the English knot.

"I have to tell you something the right way," he said, breathing heavily.

"What would be the wrong way?"

"By phone. Not that I have scruples, but yours is disconnected. TV or radio would be worse, I suppose."

"Tea?" I raised my cup.

"No thank you. May I?"

He pointed to his briefcase as if threatening to sell me something or increase the suspense about the contents inside.

"Please," I said, inviting him in.

He led me to the coffee table before stopping. The array of mother self-help material confused him. "Oh, sorry Timothy. Here, let me get these out of your way."

When I cleared it, he laid his briefcase on the table, unbuckling the locks on either side at the same time with a synchronized snap. Before lifting the top cover, he locked it again. "I'm assuming you've heard?" he asked.

"Heard?"

"Not even from family or the network?"

"What are you referring to, Timothy?"

"Your husband has been kidnapped."

The tea tasted salty to me all of a sudden, drying out my throat. I stared at the dormant television screen. My reflection stared back at me with a tinge of accusation.

"Why is your phone off?" he asked.

"The baby doesn't like it."

"Your cell?"

"I don't have one. Radiation is bad for the baby."

"Haven't you seen the news, Carol?"

"Not until nine o'clock."

"Why?"

"Too much negativity for the baby."

I stopped myself after noticing the speed of my monotone reactions. The pause stalled his momentum. His sharp-edged jaw softened into his neck, and his face transformed into a mask of concern, as if to value the way I calmed myself. He didn't realize it was a skill I practised to protect my unborn baby. However, it didn't stop him from examining me. The invisible camera in his eyes seemed to frame me, as if for the purpose of investigation. He was searching for the place where I buried the expected shock of his news, lifting veils of my bland and soft demeanour to pinpoint the source of my strength. If only he would have looked down, below my soft and motherly hair, below the glow of my skin and the swollen breasts to find the obvious—a protective womb.

He rubbed his hands together, before resuming. "You know, I was expecting to see a victim when I came here today. I thought I would have found you crying, sprawled out on the floor, vulnerable to the first shoulder, but I see something more. I know you are saddened, but I see a strong woman sitting in front of me. I see a pretty face, a relatable face, and I never noticed before how you take your time to articulate words. That's a broadcasting skill, you know, better yet, a televised interview skill. You're better than your husband, and all of us missed it."

An unexpected giggle fluttered through my lips. I was flattered by his praise, by his perception of my reaction in light of this shocking news. But I was only concentrating on what was most important to me right now, beyond my love for Paul, beyond my worries for the future, beyond the possibility of never seeing my husband again.

"We have a lot to talk about," Timothy said, unbuckling his briefcase for a second time.

"What do they want, Timothy?"

"Who?"

"The kidnappers."

"Kidnappers?"

"Yes."

"They have their requests," he said under his breath. He removed an envelope, clean and sharp with my name written on it in calligraphy.

Ignoring it, I rose from the chair to pace. The bulge of a third trimester led me to a space in the room with fresher air. Eventually, I manoeuvred my way to the kitchen to retrieve the percolating kettle. When I returned with it in hand, Timothy rose from the couch with a worried lunge. He rose from the chair to take the kettle from me, as if thinking the worst, that I would pour the boiling hot water onto myself by accident. I refused to let it go at first, but his grip on it was strong enough. I sat down again and leaned back, breathing heavily in intervals. In through my nose, out through my mouth. I could feel the shock attacking my sinuses with a dampened wind. I breathed to work against the preparation for the storm. "Yoga breathing," I repeated to myself under my breath. My hands rested on my belly, the centre of my gravity.

"You have to listen to me," Timothy said.

"What is the network doing, Timothy?"

"What they always do. Publicizing it."

My breathing increased as if in anticipation of labour pains or a contraction.

"I want to represent you," he said, removing crisp paper from the envelope.

"Me?"

"Listen to me, Carol. You can't go into war zones in your condition. But you can do more for him here. You can secure yourself and your baby."

"You represent my husband, Timothy."

"I'm still his agent, yes."

"What are you talking about then?"

"You. I want to represent you."

"Come on, Timothy. What do I have to offer?"

"Victimhood. A very marketable asset."

"Are you talking about money?"

"Yes."

"How?"

"Book deals. Television appearances. Political lobbying."

"I mean how, at this time?"

Once again, I stared at the convex mirror in the black television screen, reaching with a freshly manicured finger to press the red power button on the remote control. Locked onto the GNN channel, the screen revealed a picture of my husband next to another woman. Mug shots, except their eyes told the same story. Together, they appeared like brother and sister or husband and wife. Paul would not speak to the baby via satellite tonight. Maybe never again. Behind my cheeks, I felt the nerves loosening their foundational support of my eyes.

To distract myself from the surrender of tears, I imagined myself in the frame of the television screen, as Timothy suggested with his compliments. Comparatively, and almost competitively, would I appear as this woman appears? Her face was gaunt, but her bones were strong and sharp. A feminist if ever there was one, but definitely one not concerned about her appearance.

The very thought of achieving celebrity seemed to adjust the water in my eyes, combatting its release, as if in preparation to receive an award. How often did I walk alongside Paul as an invisible woman in the shadow of his flashes? How many times did I have to repeat my first name for people who recognized me solely as his wife? I would be a better celebrity than him, a second coming without the ego; a softer version who could appeal to the person on the other side of the screen and not just the producers, publicists, or tabloids exploiting a name.

Timothy spun his briefcase so that its insides faced me. He removed a platinum-plated pen and another contract.

"Trust me, Carol, I've been to war and back. Paul would want to hear your story. Everyone would. The story of a mother carrying the unborn child of a hero. National tension as we hope for his safe return. Good guys who look like us, bad guys with scarves and turbans. What could be better than the message of hope?"

I walked away from him again to a curtain of windows to stare out onto the Lego-like cityscape. Shiny glass buildings reflected light in the distance aside others that were dull and embedded with stone. The contrasts of time and place frightened me in the morning, the new levels building themselves up on the backs of the old.

Timothy approached me from behind, a little too closely. I could feel his wet breath on my neck, salivating. He was about to drool on my back over this opportunity. He could see the story in headlines—how he would exploit the damsel-in-distress archetype before promoting me as someone strong for that demographic of women who succumbed to afternoon soap operas and talk shows. I was a first-class talent whose rawness and naïveté could only exacerbate the cause. He could steer me into spot lit directions and create sympathy from recycled stories.

The very thought of agency, of having someone represent me, taking care of me again, but with my interests first, enticed a shiver in me. I needed to hear his support once more.

"I know it may seem wrong Carol, or contrary in nature to pursue this while Paul languishes in some hostage crisis, but contraries are the catalysts for progression. We are built in the likeness of opposites; 'attraction and repulsion, reason and energy, love and hate, are necessary for human existence to evolve.' That's just the way of the world, for better or worse."

He pointed his finger to a crane with a wrecking ball swinging between a glass building and a stone building. It swung like a pendulum marking time between two different architectural ideologies, unprepared to make a decision on its target of destruction.

He wrapped his other arm around my belly as if to know if I was crying and trying to hide it from him. When the emotion finally spread to my entire body, my belly rose and fell in his embrace, a Santa Claus jiggle but not for joy or jelly. He held me up, straight, as I threatened to keel over. My colostrum-filling breasts rested on his forearms. He secured me from falling through the window twenty-five flights down.

When I finally gained control of my own legs, my tears lightening to an aftermath of drizzle, I pressed a button on the wall and killed the classical music in the room.

CHAPTER 3: **LEA**

THEY KEPT US IN ABSOLUTE DARKNESS for a long time, until we lost track of time and sleep and day and night. I crawled about the room. Unlike my red room at the abandoned hotel, everything appeared without colour to the touch and smell and sight. They had wrapped my head in a cloth bandage made damp by the humidity. I could breathe through my mouth but not my nose.

After I woke for the first time, I could hear a man's breathing in the room. Not hurried, like the men who had rushed me here. But intermittent, with no timing or pattern. I decided it must have been Paul, so I crawled around to find him. The more I moved, the more I felt the itchiness of leftover blood on my feet and knees. I questioned if I bled anywhere else.

Chips of plaster and paint stuck to my hands, also black to my imagination. I crawled from left to right about the floor tracing his irregular breaths, but he didn't help me find him. Perhaps he couldn't feel me in the room. When they had injected me with a needle, my body chilled before reacting in a fleeting euphoric way. Perhaps he hadn't fully woken yet from his influence.

It was a pretty strong dose of something, whatever it was they injected into us. After it entered my bloodstream, it warmed my forehead to a feverish heat, eventually inspiring hallucinations of my childhood in Thorold. Back then, I was a young girl who believed in angels and spirits and curses from an evil eye. Back then, in a similar chapel darkness, I thought I heard a "calling" while I prayed in the basement of Holy Rosary Church. I wanted to tell my mother about this voice I heard. It sounded like a lover's whisper in my ear. Soft, coy, already attached to my thoughts with afterthoughts. But, back then, I was too afraid of my mother's religious zeal. It often resembled jealousy when I told her I could hear God. She accused me of being a fanatic, and then she punished me for making up stories.

So I reported my audio apparitions to the community pastor instead. Father Mazzerole chain-smoked his way around the sacristy and often left a half-smoked cigarette in the ashtray before Mass so he could finish it afterwards. He told me young girls could enter the convent but not the priesthood. Angry with him, I refused to go to church anymore.

When my father died shortly afterwards, I assumed God had punished me for praying with spite. I hated all things good and wished them buried with my father. From that point on, I challenged this God who compared his suffering on a cross with my own self-inflicted sufferings, although my body had grown immune to some, like the needles in the red room. Fortunately for me, the poison in the needles they were serving was stronger, floating me away to an acceptance of everything, even a belief in heaven again.

After all, and despite the heinous abuse on the way in, the needles were a gesture of mercy—liquid poppies. My body was accustomed to kicking back after a dosage, which was why I had woken up before Paul. He was probably in the body separation stage, still wondering whether his soul was in his body.

His breathing eventually led me to colder ground and a deep circular hole—a sewer. We were in a basement. The humidity was sharp in the air, frozen in my lungs. My hands found a cold puddle. It smelled of nothing but the cloth covering my nose, the scent of which now resembled gasoline. I licked my fingers. I tasted ammonia mixed with grime, urine perhaps. I crawled through it, and my knees stung. At that point, I realized I wasn't wearing anything but a tightly woven cloth around my head. The skin on my body was seasonal now, ice-cold in some areas and warm in others.

When I reached Paul, his feet were colder than my hands and scabbed just the same. They must have dragged him across broken glass or sharp stone on the way in. He breathed loudly through his mouth like a child pouting in a panic. Strangely enough, his legs radiated warmth. He shivered when I touched them with my wet hands.

"Paul?"

He didn't answer.

"Paul?"

He didn't inhabit his body anymore. His body had rooted itself to the cold cement like dead weight, and it breathed, but he no longer existed inside of it. With the aid of the mysterious injection, his spirit floated elsewhere in the room and did not sit up against the wall, which felt gravelly on my palm, like man-made stone or plaster.

"I'm here. Lea is here."

His senses didn't react. Not even when I took his hand and placed it on my shoulder. It rested limp enough to be dead.

"'Good is Heaven. Evil is Hell.'"

His breath finally skipped a beat when I introduced the poem he had so sarcastically quoted in our conversation at The Argument, before our capture.

I leaned in close to his ear and whispered it to his memory.

"'Then the perilous path was planted: And a river and a spring On every cliff and tomb: And on the bleachèd bones Red clay brought forth...'"

He coughed. I felt his spit on my chest as I finished:

"'Till the villain left the paths of ease, To walk in perilous paths, and drive The just man into barren climes.'"

He gripped my arm and squeezed it until it hurt so much that I had to bite my tongue. When I tore it from his grip, he spoke up from another world, where studied literature and the attempt to find meaning in it kept you up at night with existential questions.

"*'Now the sneaking serpent walks In mild humility, And the just man rages in the wilds Where lions roam.'*"

He leaned forward and vomited in my lap. I had no choice but to forgive him. I had done the same after my first time.

"THIS ISN'T MY BODY," he said, squeezing the flesh beneath his skin for a trace of sensation or workable muscle.

I could feel him in the dark room, groping for his body. I had done the same when I first woke up.

"Do you remember eating?" he asked.

"No. I rarely eat anyways."

"Do you remember sleeping?"

"I never sleep."

"Why do my legs feel like they are on the other side of the room, Lea?"

"Because they are," I answered. "Your mind has separated your soul from your body."

"*'Man has no Body distinct from his Soul,'*" he quoted out loud from the poem again, in defense, as if it held answers to life like a Bible.

"So you remember the contraries," I said, laughing, imitating the voice of our condescending professor in school, Dr. Willard.

"I feel I can hear 'The Voice of the Devil' from that poem," he said under his breath.

"Understandable. We are in Hell."

I was almost bored now with our punning of the poem.

He tried to move, and I anticipated what he would say next. "I feel paralyzed, do you?"

"You are."

"Is this blood? I feel blood."

"That's because you're bleeding."

"Are you as blind as I am?"

"If darkness is blindness, then yes."

The wrap on my head felt tighter all of a sudden. I believed that if I removed it, everything would fall out onto the floor in front of me. Brains, blood, eyes, ears, just like "Mr. Potato Head." When I breathed through my mouth, I tried hard not to swallow the suffocating scent of his vomit. I wanted to remove the wrapping, but I couldn't bring my arms up to do it. They dangled to the cold cement floor, heavy and dislocated from my body. I palmed around in the darkness for anything containing water and found a steel basin in a corner. Dragging it across the floor with one hand, I reached for the sewer with the other. When I found it, I offered the basin to Paul for him to drink. He gulped it fast, until he coughed. When he returned it to me, I drank some as well before cleansing myself of his vomit by the sewer.

"Did they rape you?" he finally asked.

"I don't think so." The question ignited a silence that ticked for hours on end, despite the absence of a clock. Time was marked only by a twitch here and there or a shared swig from the basin. There was no other change to the movement in the room. Not in the air. Not in the light. Not in my thoughts.

My mind had fixated on my daughter's birth. It took me many years to bury the memory, and like a dead body not properly cemented, it rose to the surface in that moment of absolute weakness. I remembered my husband in the hospital room writing everything down, like he was composing the original birth story. He wanted to get it down on paper, he said, every detail, for her, for us, for a future moment of reminiscence. He walked about the room recording descriptions of the wall's greenness and its chipped plaster and its worn-out leather chair. He sketched little scenes that depicted the severity of my contractions amidst the irony of the nurse's instructions. They looked at him strangely, but it didn't bother him because in his mind he was doing it for me. He was doing it to impress me so that one day we could pull out the story and recall it like a favourite poem or novel. At times, he seemed to expect acclaim for the idea, but he had only done it because his memory was never as sharp as mine. I remembered how much I hated him in that room for making the experience fictional, for stealing ownership of my pain in his feeble attempt to recreate it with words.

His story died when I gave birth. I felt emptied of the life growing within me, like I did my father's love on the day he died. And then came the news. Like water finding a crack in a wall, it broke into the void within me and filled it with an insatiable appetite for self-destruction. I could only ease its cavernous growling by inflicting pain on others or onto myself. "When they raped you, did you remove yourself from your body?"

The silence had tortured Paul enough to rephrase the question from a different angle. He had done enough interviews with rape victims to hear the same defense mechanism. However, I felt him sinister in his need to know. He craved it selfishly, to help foster him through his own self-pity.

"No." I wasn't going to give him the satisfaction. He wanted to hear I was weaker than him, unable to handle it without his questions. For someone once considered the best in the investigative journalism business, he wasn't so good or subtle at getting information out of an interviewee. Even in his capture, and faced with the prospect of death, he was greedy for a breaking news story.

"Why not?" he said, still in pursuit.

"Because I didn't want to."

I enjoyed playing the devil's advocate and the more I played, the more it confused him.

"What do you mean, Lea?"

"I said I didn't want to remove myself from my body when they raped me."

"I don't understand, Lea. What did you do?"

"I laughed hysterically."

"What did they do?"

"They stopped."

He fell silent, and I could read his mind's afterthought.

"Yes, they eventually continued," I said, resetting the lure.

"Why did you laugh in the first place?"

I had definitely confused him and took pleasure in it now. "Because I was crying so hard I found myself hearing it as laughter."

"How can that be?"

"I believed I deserved it."

"What has become of you?"

I had heard that question too many times before. It reminded me of an insistent voice echoing from the genetic hollow of my bones. The voice of my mother. After another period of suffocating silence, and despite my victory in this useless exchange, I felt the need to explain for no other reason than to dispel the quiet darkness.

"When I was younger, my mother became a religious fanatic after my father died. You know the ones who are always wearing veils in church and mumbling prayers to themselves through their blackened teeth? She would only kneel on the cement floor, never on the kneeler, and she would pray one hundred rosary decades a day. Her rosary was heavy steel with sharp crystal beads that wrapped around her hand tightly, like a choke collar. The religious pictures in our home were bloody, all of them. We had a picture of the face of Jesus with his crown of thorns, and his entire face dripped red with blood. My mother once told a priest he would go to Hell if he placed communion in someone's palm. She dragged me to church every morning and every night, and when I refused one beautiful spring day, on the anniversary of my father's death, she told me I wasn't worthy. That only the good suffer."

"Is that it? Are you suffering to be good again? Is that how you explain this?"

"Me? I am furthest from good. I am everything I despise and love at the same time."

"You belong here," he said, giving up again.

I believed the interview went well.

A WHITE SPOTLIGHT BLINDED ME, and I barely noticed when a pair of hands grabbed me from behind and tore the head-wrap off of my face. I couldn't see anything but light and shards of reflecting glass. Someone behind me jammed a cover over my nakedness. It smelled of sack and bark. I could not see Paul, but he was there.

"Lea?"

Someone clubbed him over the head for seeking me out. I shivered at the sound of breaking bone.

Shadows emerged in the room as my focus sharpened. We were in a dream, and the setting was a stage. Or a set for a television show. I couldn't tell yet.

I stared face to face at a video recorder on a tripod. Spotlights hung above it on thin black stands. To the left, a sphere with an eye dangled from a loose wire. The cord hung in the air like a clothesline. It led to a portable computer like mine. Behind the computer, a smaller, thinner man typed away before getting up and rewiring something. I had recognized young eyes above a scarf before, but he wasn't Adnan. This young boy's eyelashes were long and curly, almost primped. Like the others, he moved with determination, except his gestures indicated expertise instead of menace. He was here only to arrange the shiny equipment in place. The ground beneath my feet had changed from that in the basement. I stood on cloth now. It spread without pattern on the floor, like spilled paint.

The lens of the video recorder rounded in and out and pointed at me like the firearms behind it. Lots of them crowded the room this time. They stood covering the wall in a firing line behind the white spotlights and underneath them. Their faces were veiled entirely, even their chins and necks. I couldn't see Paul yet, until two hands pressed my shoulders down. I slipped to a sitting position on the cloth. He sat next to me. The shadows bubbling below the surface of his face had turned a shade of green in the brightness.

A director's guttural, Arabic voice commanded our attention from behind the camera. He sounded confused. The young boy ran over to the camera to offer him a few pointers, before he returned to the computer. I could hear the *tap tap* of his typing on the keyboard. The camera crept closer to us as if to prey upon our white blindness. I felt a pistol point pushing into and almost through my temple. It remained there, piercing my skin with its sharper tunnel end like a tiny tube about to suck out the contents of my skull with one flick of a switch.

"You will read." The young one from behind the computer spoke with accented English. I assumed he was the only one in the room who could speak English.

The pistol point resumed its enforcing role, this time pointing a line of vision to the cue cards. A young boy's penmanship had printed the English words, big and round enough for me to read clearly. In my periphery, I saw Paul's head pointed to the same target. A red light atop the camera flashed in intervals while a beeping noise sounded to prepare the performance for real time.

The gun at his head nudged Paul to read first. I read along silently to myself.

"*We are not terrorists. We are political artists of torture. We have kidnapped your journalists and we will inflict our will on them if our demands are not met.*"

I felt the coldness of the gun rest against my face while they spoke.

"*With your bombs, you have destroyed our temples of culture. With your rockets, you have inflamed our books and burned our history. With your ideologies, you have smeared our way of life and polluted our language. With your planes, you have stained our views of the sky. You have made morgues of our mosques.*"

The cue-card holder scrambled the sheets to find the right one. He looked back for a signal from the director.

"Remove your soldiers from our places of culture. If not, we will create tortures that will cleanse the medium between our worlds and herald a new age of death."

Paul paused before he read the next line to look at me. The gun, previously used as a conductor's baton to direct various sections of an orchestra, now pointed deep into his temple. I understood why he had risked a glance. In his eyes, I could read the realization that this medium summarized us. We were journalists that altered the perception of these people and the war with our words. We were the symbols for this medium. We needed to suffer for things to become cleansed, infinite again. When Paul refused to say the next line, the gun at my temple pressed in like a knife as a reminder to speak up.

"Please save us."

The spotlights sucked in their own light, revealing a red core that refused to cool down without some time. The men in the room congratulated themselves with hugs, all except for the young boy at the computer. He continued to type away as if racing to an end he could only reach on his own. In the meantime, the director of the show slowly approached to applaud his actors. He grabbed the gun from a man's hand, turned it around and smashed the handle into Paul's face. I felt wetness on the side of my face and a tooth under my foot when they led me back to the room in the basement. The floors there were cold cement and slippery, but it didn't matter after the injection.

CHAPTER 4: CAROL

I SAT IN FRONT OF A MIRROR with eight round bulbs protruding in a line above it. I counted them. Once. Twice. In reverse. Over and over again. They buzzed bright, and I could see the curled coils beneath the glass. A tableau of crouched figures reflected in the mirror behind me, their heads bobbing. Timothy Abel stood above them, talking into his hand, or rather, the phone hidden in his palm.

A woman dusted my cheek while another straightened my hair with electrical prongs. I could smell skunk as my burning hair mixed with the powder in the air. Another woman clumped a slab of concealer on my face and didn't smooth it out. I wondered if the makeup artist had applied so much after noticing my facial swelling. Although I had spent the better part of my nights training myself not to cry, I couldn't help myself from waking with puffy eyes. Paul was away in a desert, captured, on death row in a place I advised him not to explore for stories. What kind of man abandons his family, a baby he has not met yet, to chase what he could easily borrow or fictionalize? He never listened to me and despite what *The Expectant Mother* book advised, that my baby could feel my tears, I couldn't control their release, the way they flushed the violent melancholy that had attacked me when I first received news of Paul's kidnapping from Timothy.

"It will give you angles. Don't worry," the makeup artist said, flattening the slab out, but not smoothly, on my jawline.

I believed this stranger understood me more than my own husband. Or was I simply experiencing another level of grief, like blame? *First comes sadness, then comes anger, then comes a baby in a single-mother carriage.*

I rested my trembling hands on my belly to calm them down. They agreed to lower the news desk for me, just as Timothy requested. It would reveal the earth below my breasts, wrapped in an aquamarine blue dress that sparkled like sun on the ocean.

"Are you nervous?" Timothy asked from behind me again. He always snuck up on me from behind.

"No."

"Do you want to review the questions?" he asked.

"Not really."

"Just remember, take your time. You don't want to sound like you've rehearsed it. You want to come across as articulate but stunted in your obvious worry. Remember, we want to give your audience a visual of pity to create the 'poor, abandoned mother effect,' but we also want to exploit the options provided by your ability to talk intelligently about the situation. This will attract buyers for your story, which in turn, will redefine you as a multi-faceted celebrity."

"Celebrity?"

"Yes, every celebrity needs a 'rags-to-riches' story to sell the dream. Right now, you're at the rags stage, but I'm going to raise you to the riches. Trust me."

I couldn't help to admire Timothy's reflection in the mirror. Tanned a new shade of orange for the day, he would appear beside me for support, as a friend of my husband's, as the creator of my celebrity. Not Paul's agent, but the man who could mix the ingredients of curiosity, timing, and manipulation as a recipe for interest in me. No man ever tried to improve my status this way before. No man could ever pull off the miracle of resurrecting these selfish dreams and make me feel good about it at the same time, even in the midst of the greatest tragedy of my life. One of the makeup ladies followed him around as if expecting a treat. Another older man with shimmering white hair and a perfectly trimmed moustache spoke to my reflection in the mirror. His silky chin touched the exposed skin on my left shoulder.

"Paul might hear you, you know."

I didn't answer him. He disappeared behind the woman straightening my hair. When he reappeared, he moved closer and his face expanded larger in the mirror. His voice resembled my father's, strong and assured in its delivery, but more deliberate than my memory of him.

"I want you to meet our other guest on the show."

The man standing next to Patrick Ridgeway, my interviewer, resembled a mannequin. His skin was painted in beautifully toned strokes on the canvas of his flawless face, while his bright blue eyes shimmered like shine lines in a sapphire. His soft handshake warmed my hand. "It's an honour to meet you, Mrs. Shell."

He didn't mention his name. He assumed I recognized him from a late night alone in front of Channel 39. I did. *The* Robert Risi, a famous actor and mediocre singer was interested in meeting me. Little old me! Well into a sales pitch, he spoke to me as if to suggest he needed me more than I admired him.

"I recently released a country and western CD. I'm planning to promote it and raise money for my own charity that supports the war efforts overseas. It's called, *Performers in Iraq.* I've created this foundation that supports talented actors or performers who are presently serving in Iraq and can't audition for roles here until they return. We don't want them to lose their chance at work, or a chance at fame, because of the war."

I lost my train of thought after the word '*war.*' Some aesthetic artist had edged and pencilled his eyebrows in so perfectly. He paused, as if to question my observatory lock on him. "Hold on. Okay, I know what you're thinking, Mrs. Shell."

"What's that?"

"You're thinking, what is a Jewish-Italian actor from New

York trying to prove by going country? Let me tell you, I'm quite the hybrid of influences. Do you realize there's also a little hip hop in my country and western? If you listen to it closely, you'll hear its cadences working against the acoustics. It's a marvellous mix."

"Wow. I would have never thought." I did my best to feign a new interest, while he talked his way around my impenetrable stare. I tried hard to look away, I really did, but he was too glossy and golden to look elsewhere. His absolute perfection hypnotized me into trying to find a flaw somewhere. I had read an article about Rick Moody, the American author who happened to visit the movie set where Ang Lee was adapting his novel into film. Amongst other boring observations, he couldn't help but be fascinated by how beautiful the actors were. Here was a sound academic completely overwhelmed by the superficial beauty of actors. He couldn't work his mind around it, and here I was, imagining Robert Risi in my romantic embrace.

"I would love for you to join our walk against violence at the Prayer and Protest Festival." He handed me a card with the name of a woman and a number.

"Rita is my publicist. Have your person call mine."

He left, shaking hands with Timothy on his way out.

His absence reminded me of the embarrassment of having a slab of concealer on the side of my face where he spoke to me, although he didn't seem to notice it. He interviewed first, with a slab of his own that I could detect in its application from off the set. As I watched him interview, his melodic voice inspired the baby to kick, so I walked back into the wings to avoid ruining my dress with a hormonal accident.

Were these new pregnancy hormones, I thought to myself, as I walked with my legs apart, or was I realizing the infinite possibilities of my new celebrity about to take flight after this interview? Timothy had assured me I would need a security detail after this interview. This was my coming out party, so to speak. This interview would make me recognizable around the world. It would open every door, according to Timothy, and not just one with a fifteen -minute time limit. My celebrity would endure, like Princess Diana's, he claimed.

I returned to the set after cooling down from my hot flash. I would try harder not to focus on Robert Risi. I would have to learn how to act like a celebrity if I was to become one. I would have to teach myself not to show excitement, or attraction for that matter, in the presence of another one. I would have to pretend myself to be the most interesting and sought-after person in the room. This would take an adjustment, of course. I was never the most important person in the room with Paul. Camera flashes always sought him out with hurried journalists chasing him behind the light with questions. And like an idiot, I stood in his shadow, always with a toothy smile, my arms tightening around his elbow, his biggest supporter should he ever decide to enter a political race one day.

He often spoke out loud about such aspirations while he dressed into his pyjamas before bed. He needed a sounding board for his dreams, a human mirror for himself. He needed to hear me say, "Yes," no matter how ridiculous the idea. "Yes, honey, I can see you as the president of the United States one day;" and "Yes, another network would pay you double what you are making at GNN;" and "Yes, you should go back to Iraq because it would reignite your comeback;" and "Yes, it's all right that you leave your pregnant wife to chase a story because why not, you're Paul Shell and everyone wants to be you on television."

God forbid I said no. That would mean I alter the rotation of the earth or the orbit circling his star. I found myself inching closer and closer to the news desk, instinctively. And for the first time at the studio, I realized how small his world really was, how tiny the set he launched his fame from. Encased in a small, grungy room with a thousand spotlights hanging from a grid of metal bars, I now tiptoed on his televised hallowed ground. One wall exposed a tapestry with a phony city skyline. Coloured cords and wires funnelled above the grid like muscle strands on an anatomy chart. Below the desk, where I would sit, cement plastered the ground. Tape crosses and chalk numbers reserved angle spots for the cameras. They crept closer and closer to the conversation. Men with shaky arms held boom microphones high above. I could read the teleprompter. Although I had visited the place where my husband worked, I never viewed a live broadcast or an interview. I had always been outside the glass door, not inside the bubble. Patrick Ridgeway, the interviewer with the brilliant white hair and moustache, spoke with my father's tone of voice again.

"So what do you think about the war, Robert?"

"The war has been put there for us to defeat. It's a test, Patrick, to further our country's greatness in history."

"But is the enemy defeatable, Robert? Do you think we will emerge victorious in the end?"

"If we show reason in the face of adversity, Patrick."

"Reason, Robert?"

"A wise man once said, and let me tell you, I've used it as a lyric in one of my songs, that '*Reason is the bound or outward circumference of Energy.*'"

"Sounds like an interesting quote, Robert. Who is this wise man?"

"Well, Patrick, that wise man would be Robert Blake."

"So, if I am hearing you correctly, you are saying that we have to answer their passionate energy for war with our conservative reason for peace to emerge victorious, to conquer terrorism?"

"Precisely, Patrick."

"Reason and Energy. I never thought of it that way," Patrick said, sitting back with a satisfied grin.

"Reason is the key, the new slogan for this war," Robert said, like 'Give peace a chance." "On that poignant note," Patrick said, transitioning, "we'll be back with the wife of kidnapped journalist Paul Shell."

The red light flashed on, but not to signal any emergency. Patrick spoke to a woman with giant headphones approaching the elevated dais.

"Sharpen it for God's sake, we need more treble."

"Thank you, Patrick; I'll leave this right here." Robert stood up, shaking hands with his interviewer, simultaneously leaving his CD behind. He walked by me with a smile and a blink of the right eye. The soles of my feet, arched by my heels, seemed to ooze out from my shoes. A stagehand placed another seat next to Patrick. The makeup artist touched him up while an intern holding a clipboard escorted Timothy and me to our seats. The cameras retreated. When the red light flickered, they bounced like insects on their suspended cranes. I sat closer to Patrick, the interviewer. His breath was smokey under a cloak of mint. Timothy rolled his chair closer to me, auditioning poses, his hand on my shoulder. His hand on the table. His hand on the back of my seat. He settled for that position.

"In five, four, three, two, one."

"Welcome back. Before we move on, the CD is titled *Reason and Energy* and the artist is Robert Risi of course, from the hit television series *Angels of War*. Now, ladies and gentleman, we have a special guest in the studio."

One of the cameras intersected the path of another. It made its way to a blue-taped cross on the floor. In the reflection of the lens, I could see Timothy striking a pose with his serious face. The camera crept closer and closer. I was afraid it would never stop. I reminded myself not to flinch. It crept closer until it switched to my interviewer.

"Mrs. Shell, we can't imagine what you must be feeling at this moment."

The camera nearly climbed on the desk now. It lowered to focus on the profile of my belly, before it rose to my face.

"I'm still in shock, Patrick."

"It's beyond reason what is happening to your husband, our very own Paul Shell."

"Yes, it is."

"Tell us, what is being done to bring him home, Carol?"

I remembered this question from the sheet of paper, although my nerves created a blockage, preventing an answer from reaching my tongue, almost causing me to blank out with an aneurysm.

"There are many support groups working hard to bring Paul home." It was a lie, but I believed it in front of the camera.

"Do you think you will ever see him again, Carol?"

Another camera left Patrick's angle to assume a second on my profile. A side profile of my face. I sat back trying hard to ignore its prompt to smile. Timothy warned me to restrain myself, to refrain from revealing any indication of happiness, especially in the light of this attention, which would seem contrived to a televised audience. He explained how certain facial emotions and reactions communicated different meanings when filmed. Like arrogance instead of confidence. Or drunkenness instead of sadness. Timothy advised me to focus on the key word: *pity*. "Feel sorry for yourself," he said, "and it will show on your face." Such a hard task against the flattery of this bright attention. The cameras fought over me.

"Yes. I know I will see him again, Patrick. I can feel it right here," I pointed to my heart and then, in an inspired moment of improvisation, I placed my hand on my belly, "and right here."

Patrick nodded while his face creased into a sincere oil painting. Timothy spoke up beside me.

"Everything humanly possible is being done to extricate Paul Shell from this unfortunate situation. If you can hear us Paul, we're in your corner, my friend."

He swung his arm around me. An older, unshaven man with a clipboard behind the camera waved it off. Timothy dropped it to the seat again.

I proceeded with my co-written plea. "Please. If you are detaining Paul, don't hurt him. He is a man, he is my husband, and he is the father of my baby." I paused, remembering

Timothy's words about dramatic effect. I could hear Timothy's voice inside my inner ear, like it was being transmitted. At the same time, I could see my invisible audience, hanging on every "live" word.

"With him, we are a family. Without him, we are alone."

A white handkerchief emerged from the light, descending like a dove into the hand of my interviewer. I grasped for it not knowing which eye the tear escaped from. Before I could raise it to my face, the cameras retreated, bent over and collapsed as if from exhaustion. Patrick coughed, stood upright from his chair and shouted.

"Makeup!"

A few of the headphone people huddled around the desk supplying me with bubbly water and a fresh handkerchief. Timothy stepped aside to answer a phone call.

The lights dimmed. A digital clock stopped keeping time above the exit door. I sat alone, behind the desk as my husband once did, realizing I had nailed my opportunity to speak to the world, but I failed to say anything about the woman kidnapped along with my husband.

CHAPTER 5: LEA

A MAN IN A SCARF LEFT US A BOOK beside the square plate of food. He set it in a corner of the room next to a slice of carpet. He locked the door on the other side, and the sound of a chain knocked against it.

"Don't go near it. It's a trap or poison," Paul cautioned.

I crawled to it. When I arrived to the scent of the spot, I felt the leather cover of the book first before dipping my fingers into the dark mush. It tasted of corn. My stomach was starved, too sore to accept it. It dripped back onto the plate from my swollen fingertips, and I returned once again to the book. Its worn texture reminded me of the prayer book in my bathroom. The one I stored my needle in.

"It's a book of proverbs, I believe. A religion of hieroglyphics."

I couldn't read in the dark, but I could discern bold lines of print engraved into the page as if from a stone chisel.

"Leave it be," Paul snarled under his breath.

I gripped the book like a wheel. I knew it would annoy him, even if I faked a reading of it.

"This is the story of red and green, of two starving journalists in the dark seeking a light. Voices in the wilderness. A man and a woman shivering by a sewer."

"I told you to leave it be, Lea."

Paul bandaged his stomach with one arm. The other appeared lifeless astride his body, disjointed from his shoulder. We had not eaten for days, maybe weeks, possibly years in our minds.

He often clenched parts of his body as if to prevent them from inducing an appetite in the others as yet unscathed. "They are going to kill us soon," he said.

"I don't feel that way. Here, try this."

I pushed the plate of food at him. He tasted it, but his body rejected it in the same way mine did. He spat it out with a violent cough.

"Why are they letting us rot?" he asked.

"To prepare us."

"For what?"

"For film."

"For film?"

"Yes. They need us to deteriorate. It's symbolic to them, this process of torture, and the recording of it. It's an act of purification," I explained.

"What are they purifying?" Paul asked.

"Our corruption. They fear turning into us the same way we fear turning into them."

"But why not kill us outright and make the statement?"

"Because they don't believe in elimination. They believe in revision. They need to reveal how much weaker we are. They need to prove to the world that they can evoke change with more fear. We are visual text to them, portraits to lend credibility to their religious science."

I flipped through the pages, squinting to read anything with a message. My knuckles throbbed. Humidity had infiltrated the spaces between my joints. My hands bubbled blue in the darkness, and some of my nails had eroded away into swollen stubs, although their sensitive touch remained. The sound of the page flipping annoyed him even further.

"I will never convert," he said. His tone was final.

I refused to answer him. Everything he said spouted from his mouth like a burst of steam. He coughed more often, and his knees shivered some nights. The previous night I made my way over to him to share my warmth, but he kicked me away.

I liked him only after an injection. He was better with opiates floating in his blood.

When I heard the rattling of keys at the door again, I dropped the book and scurried to the other side of the room. A group of them entered in a knot that began unravelling in different directions. One held a heated spotlight in his hand. It revealed the room to me. Nail-scratched walls. Wavy slopes in the cement floor. Dangling chains resembling sleeping snakes on a branch tied to a beam holding up the ceiling. Two steel doors locked with rusted padlocks. The man with the scarf pulled an electrical cord into the room. Another man yanked a second orange cord through. He had something in his hand, but he held it behind his back. I could feel the same warmth as the spotlight emanating from behind him. The warmth made the walls creak and the floor crack.

Another hunched man walked in with a short stool and a book under his arm. He searched for a particular spot in the room. When he found it, he sat there sharpening a pencil with a knife. In the light, I could see his tan, wrinkled skin above the scarf. He was old and frail. He began to draw.

Paul pressed his back into the gravelly wall before covering his eyes with shaky arms. The light and the organization of this visit maddened him more than my fake reading. The portable spotlight moved, and a wall of light erased the darkness as it descended upon me. It was so bright that I couldn't see Paul anymore, but I could hear him shouting out loud.

"Leave us alone!"

A red dot spotted the bright white light, floating like a firefly in the room. Two sets of hands, one on either side of me, lifted me to the standing position as they did Paul.

"What are you doing to her?" he demanded, but they avoided his questions as if to suggest he spoke a dialect of fear they couldn't understand or interpret. Paul could see it and feel the warmth from whatever it originated. His face melted into a scowl, disgusted by its apparent threatening suggestion.

At once, one man spun me around so that my back faced him.

I could hear the wooden sticks breaking over Paul to quiet him. Some struck hard bones and made a blunt sound.

I assumed they were going to rape me again, the whole group of them this time, but they tightened their grips on my legs instead in order to plant them firmly in a rooted place. The warmth became heat and the heat became a flame as it pressed into my back.

I didn't want to scream, but this time I couldn't help myself. The rest of my body retreated in a shiver and then magnetized to the hot flat iron sizzling the skin on my right shoulder. My legs were held down by the ankles and they shook violently as if to wriggle out of their restraints. My spine curved to slide away, but the iron stayed there. To the right of my face, being pressed into the gravelly wall, I saw the outline of a lens. Behind it seared the warmth of the spotlight. In the light, I could see the young boy's eyelashes behind the camera. He was filming me. Paul remained quiet or dead or gagged. When they removed the iron from my back, I collapsed onto the floor. When I did so, a man injected me in the arm with a needle. It struck bone, and I convulsed when the heat radiating from my shoulder touched the cold cement ground. Through a sheath of blurred vision, I could see the young boy taking pictures of me as if at a photo shoot, snapping away at various angles. Why had he taken such an interest in my pain? He was snapping away while the others yelled at him in Arabic tongues to shift his attention to Paul. At one juncture, he had hurried up to me to move my arm aside, capturing the barest hint of what must have been a defiant stare.

I was a model of torture for him. A subject of implicit meaning. A stilled visual with a message. But there was something more in his obsession, a passion for the art of capturing. The boy photographer with the long eyelashes knew that my pain was flashing and would be gone in a brief moment, and he was determined to capture that moment. Joel had told me once that there was an art to capturing someone in a frame. At just the right moment of light and darkness, you could capture the contrary nature of the human condition. This was what they'd meant by calling themselves, "artists of torture."

In-between strobe-lit flashes I could see Paul screaming in flickering frames. His mouth was agape again, the darkened gums below the bottom row of his teeth showing as he faced the iron. They pressed the flat iron to the region thinly covering his heart. He was biting his tongue or his lip, and I could hear the snapping crunch as he bit too hard. He eventually dropped to the ground and flopped like fish emptied from a net.

I managed to move an inch, but my melted skin stuck to the floor. It tore another ounce of pain from the inside of my chafing throat. I tried to talk as the heroin waved through my veins in search of an oasis. Cold and heat. Heat and cold. My voice garbled out spit. Unintelligible words, which held buried memories treasured and regretted at the same time. I recalled anything to distract my softening mind from the needles of pain induced by the hot flat iron. I thought of desperate times. My childhood before my father died. The way my tiny hand tickled his scratchy palm. It didn't help. I recalled the first time I made love to a boy at Watasatchin camp in a small tent and how he let me lie on top of him all night to avoid the cold ground. This memory offered little relief to the area of my body the drugs couldn't penetrate for the life of them.

I thought of the phrase, "corroding fires," and for a moment, I was relieved by the revelation of a young girl who missed her father lighting birthday candles with a match. How he burned himself repeatedly to illuminate the entire cake. The glow of fire on her face. The same young girl who hated taller people laughing over stained plates and drinks after his funeral, shattering a wall sconce by accident, or so she told her mother. The young girl who could never find any birthday light in the pure darkness after his death, until

CHAPTER 6: CAROL

THE MAN AT MY DOOR introduced himself as a ghost. "Timothy Abel sent me. My name is Conrad Spector."

"Why did he send you?" Carol asked.

"He wants me to put your story to print."

"Story?"

"Well, part story, part memoir, part fiction." He started to laugh.

I let him in.

Channel 41 had taken the television set hostage. Since my husband's kidnapping, I had left it on at every minute of the day. Every once in a while, Paul would speak from a previous recording or a past assignment. I would run up and stand on a chair so that my belly leaned against the speaker. Sporadically, they looped my interview with the silver moustache, Patrick Ridgeway. I watched it many times over. And the more I scrutinized it, the more I fell in love with this version of myself. The forlorn wife of a journalist left abandoned by homeland security. The accessible hero and everywoman. Mother, wife, and independent homemaker who was educated, pretty, stylish, and strong.

I searched for any basis of criticism, but I could not find anything to point to as I watched myself bloom on the screen. A few times, I actually laughed at the image of my face, perfectly angled by the camera shot—the smudge of concealer on my jawline invisible to my audience. The makeup crew did wonders with my face's presentation. I appeared angelic and maternal at the same time, almost virginal. I was already imagining myself as an icon in front of the camera. I couldn't help it. I had finally walked upon stage.

"This kitchen table is fine," Conrad Spector said, assuring me without an invitation to set up shop there.

He stalled after he removed his laptop and file folders from a briefcase.

"Your name again, sir?"

"My name is Conrad Spector, but you can call me 'Ghost,' if you like. Short for 'Ghostwriter,' which is what I do, what I am, and what most of my close friends call me."

"Mr. Spector?"

"That will work too."

"Would you like some tea, Mr. Spector?" I pointed to the stainless steel rack near the stove that housed my collection.

"I much prefer coffee or alcohol if you have it."

"How about both?"

"Just what the doctor ordered."

I pressed the automatic espresso machine on the counter. It gurgled beans, made a moaning sound, crushed them into sand, and then released its tarry stream into a small cup. The cap of the liqueur bottle was dried stuck, and I had to force it open. The sugar had melted and congealed into the grooves, gluing it tight. Spector rose to help me with it. He poured more into the cup than I expected. It scented the air.

"Forgive my rudeness," he said.

"Not a problem."

He escorted me back to the table with his soft, wrinkly hand. He was a young man with ghastly features. Liver-spotted hands, loose skin on his neck. A pointed chin as if to suggest that some of the bone had been removed. Sunken black eyes and whispery light hair.

"I'm a survivor," he said, clearly feeling the need to explain after catching me in the act of observation.

"Whatever do you mean, Mr. Spector?"

"Do you know what you are looking at, Mrs. Shell?"

"Sorry, I lost myself."

"It's all right. I said I am a survivor. Several different cancers. Just finished another round of chemo. This time, I lost my taste buds and everything I touch gives me a shock. But I'm beginning to eat without tasting metal and to feel without electricity running through my veins, of course."

As his skeletal fingers dripped like melting icicles from his wrists onto the keyboard, it seemed inevitable that the enemy lurked elsewhere where he hadn't yet searched, waiting for him to fall asleep before a last minute attack. The keys clicked softly.

"Okay. How are we going to do this, Mrs. Shell?"

I lost all focus. I was staring beyond him now, almost through him, and out the window. The wrecking ball slammed into the modern glass building and not the old stone, as I first suspected. The future shattered to shiny pieces, glittering in the sunlight as it fell to the ground; the past remained in character, unshakeable.

"Mrs. Shell?"

"Yes, sorry. What does a ghostwriter do again, Mr. Spector?"

He lowered the screen.

"Just as the name suggests. I am going to write your story in your words. The name on the book will be yours, but I will have written it."

"Why?"

"Why am I writing it, or why write the story?"

"Both, I suppose."

"Timothy selected me from those who applied for the job. I gave him my payment conditions, and we signed a contract. As for the story, there is a lot of interest at the moment. Timothy has three major publishers lined up, and he will set up an auction for the work. We need to get started on the proposal. First, we compile notes. We write an outline, a synopsis, a platform. Then, a few chapters."

"A few chapters?"

"Yes, that's another reason why Timothy hired me. I create stories; I don't simply record them, Mrs. Shell."

"You create them, even if they are truth in their own right?"

"Most especially if they are true. That's my specialty. I make the truth come to life."

"With what, if I may ask, Mr. Spector?"

"With lies, of course. And language. I'm a writer, Mrs. Shell. A cabinet without finishing is simply a box of wood in its true form. I stylize and customize. I make the truth more true."

He reached into his briefcase to remove some samples. Each boasted a bestseller epigram atop the title. One of them featured a golden "Oprah's Book Club" sticker. His name was invisible on the cover, but I could feel his presence in one that I took in my hand, like his spirit churned inside of it.

"My specialty is celebrity memoirs, Mrs. Shell."

I deduced that much from the familiarity of names and pictures on the covers of his books. I imagined myself on the cover of one, in a comfortable pose. Never in my life did I envision my image gracing the cover of a book in a store. The whole notion of it suggested immortality and then fear. My life story was generic until Paul's kidnapping. What could I possibly offer before this crisis? My mundane, sheltered life as a privileged schoolgirl, whose parents practically arranged her marriage through mutual friends and business contacts. I was almost embarrassed to reveal any of that material to the ghost. He would laugh at the absence of conflict and the obvious presence of coddling and security. Both of my parents were still alive and retired. I quit my private school teaching job when I became pregnant, and not because I couldn't work. I didn't feel it necessary and I simply knew I could.

"I understand what you may be thinking, that no one will want to read about you, am I correct, Mrs. Shell?"

I stared at him horrified. Was I that predictable?

"That's where I come in. You will tell me about your life

and your husband's life and then your life together and I will make you into a heroine of your generation. The power of language is insurmountable. It can deify and humble you at the same time."

The television in the adjoining room increased in volume on its own. The news reporter usurped the screen for an update.

"This just in, General Riddick of the First Armoured Division is here to discuss progress from the very bowels of the war on terrorism."

A man decorated in spots with a square hat and hard, tanned skin stood upright at attention. Behind him, sand drifted and blurred the screen.

"Our soldiers are making a strong stand against the enemy. They are fighting in guerrilla warfare conditions to reduce insurgent violence in other areas. We have declared another victory, and glory has been achieved. Now we have work to do in order to *secure* our victory."

"What do you make of the recent kidnappings of journalists; in particular, our own Paul Shell?"

A pale picture of my husband floated into the corner of the screen, his name scrawled underneath.

"It's a catch-twenty-two. The majority of journalists reside in the green zone where they are protected from any danger. We have not lost a journalist in the green zone. However, the stories are limited from behind these walls and some journalists have risked their lives to venture out into the red zone. I can't speak for this risk, but I can say that we are doing our best to protect those troubadours of free speech who stay within our boundaries."

"Thank you General Riddick."

With the prompting of a studio saxophone, the screen cut to a retirement investment commercial. I was angry with the picture of my husband. The network neglected to tell me he had ventured into the red zone. Had he gone to meet this woman who was captured with him? Where were his priorities with this risk? Did I mean so little to him back home? He never valued or felt the need to protect me when he resided with me. He left me often to chase a story, sometimes with the door unlocked. Timothy would never leave me so vulnerable, so unsafe. He took every effort to strengthen my image, improve upon my flaws, and protect his investment. He focused on my well-being, whereas Paul considered me complementary, like a necessary but bland background or a seldom worn, out-of-season, but still attractive leather jacket.

"Mrs. Shell? Do you want to start from the beginning and make our way to the day you found out about the kidnapping?"

"No, Mr. Spector."

"No?"

"I want to start from right now, in the present. I want to tell you how it feels to have a baby growing inside of me while my husband is looking for boxes of wood in Iraq."

The ghostwriter pulled in his elbows and rested his palms on a pad before the keyboard. His face, skull-like with its translucent sheath of skin, turned to the screen, and I some-how felt I could trust him to write a story that would be both memorable and fancy.

CHAPTER 7: LEA

PAUL'S INCESSANT MOANING replaced the music of his breathing, and I was not happy about the change. The back of my shoulder felt like it was leaking fluid down the crane of my spine, and it wasn't blood. It felt thinner, cleaner. Paul curled up in a corner, shivering to make it go away.

"Please, another needle. Please," he repeated over and over again as if his captors presided over him like nurse administrators.

I made my way over to him again. As I did so, I felt the burnt skin on my back tear. An explosion of nerve endings tingled to the edges of my scalp like ingrown horns.

"Stay away from me," Paul said, pushing me away with his voice. He had lost all trust in anyone else, except himself.

I didn't say anything. When I came close enough to hear his body heaving those moans, I tried to touch him. He slapped me away.

"I don't want you near me."

So I sat there for a while, invisible, close to him. I could hear him whispering something to himself. The same words repeated in a cyclical rhythm. He was praying. Maybe praying to keep everything away, even me. I decided to leave him with his privacy. I crawled over to the prayer carpet our captors had left as a reminder of conversion. I remembered having seen it in the light, its floral design. When I reached it, I took hold of the book resting on it. He heard me flipping through the

pages, and this annoyed him. "That's the Devil's book, Lea."
"It's a Book of Proverbs, I told you. Or at least, I think it is."
"Yeah, Proverbs from Hell."

Every word of his carried a smoking trail of anger. I purposely flipped the pages to annoy him. It was still too dark in
the room to translate the symbols, and I wondered why our
captors would plant an illegible book in the cell. Did they believe that it carried a power beyond its words? That its hidden
contents could baptize us into conversion? Although I could
not determine the language, I could distinctly see that it was
written in separate lines, not paragraphs, like a poem, or a list
of rules. It could have been the Book of Life for all I knew.

I could smell the aftermath of our skin charring in the absolute darkness. Paul resumed his moaning again. His prayers
couldn't distract him from the pain for too long. To appease
him, I recited lines from the poem we voluntarily memorized
for a crazy professor in school who cared for nothing else
in his life. And I knew too well that Paul couldn't resist the
challenge of answering my memory with his. At the very least,
it would mobilize his anger. We needed the poetry of "The
Marriage of Heaven and Hell" in different ways. Me, for my
sanity. He, for relief.

"*In seed time learn, in harvest teach, in winter enjoy,*" I
began.

His moaning ceased before he spoke in retaliation. "*Dip
him in the river who loves water.*"

"*Drive your cart and your plough over the bones of the
dead,*" I said.

He released a sigh after this line, so I repeated it again. "*Drive
your cart and your plough over the bones of the dead.... He
whose face gives no light, shall never become a star.*"

His voice was alive now, and his pronunciation of the line ex-
act: "*Prudence is a rich, ugly old maid courted by Incapacity.*"

He laughed and I laughed and we were mad with the juice
of the poem.

As if cued by the last line, the heat of the spotlight emerged outside the door again. Our captors had heard our laughter. It indicated healing, freedom of mind, or the release of spirit. I snatched the book when a ray of light lasered a path under the door and onto the floor. It revealed the empty basins of water alongside the wall and the plate of food. Old china with a traditional floral design on its outer edges. The set resembled one from my grandmother's buffet table. It was as if they had stolen it from my memory, as if to remind me on purpose of the time when I broke one by accident and had to piece it together with glue so that I wouldn't be caught.

I balanced myself on my knees, and when the door broke open, the spotlight revealed me praying to the camera. Paul was bruised in the light. I could see that they had branded the cross on his chain into his chest. It was white and bubbly in that area, almost shining in its outline. Definitely a third degree burn or worse. He hated me with a death stare at that moment, like I had sold him the torture I was supposed to receive. The men in scarves stopped when they realized I was praying with their book in my hands. However, their hesitation dissipated when they remembered the laughter that required punishing.

Another man snapped a whip when he walked into the room. His shadow was menacing enough to force Paul into the shell of his crouched limbs.

This foreman ordered the men to restrain us. A group of others filed in like soldiers, including the young boy with the camera slung over his shoulders. Two of them sat on my knees and nearly broke them backwards with their weight while the boy snapped shots. The older sketch artist took up a stool and scratched away in a book. Was he drawing us, or the scene, and to what purpose when we were already captured on film? The man with the whip tested it on the cement floor next to my ear. It echoed and reverberated like a distorted twang from an electric guitar.

A knee over my neck kept my head down, restricting my vision to the lit ceiling. I could see solid beams of steel running like railway tracks over the stone wall and across to other rooms. There was dark blood smeared up high on the walls. How could it have reached such a height? The two men sitting on my knees pulled my toes back against the bone of my shin.

The sting of the whip sliced the bottoms of my feet with the same heat from the flat iron. My body recognized it and threatened to catch fire. I screamed and then Paul screamed and then I screamed and then Paul screamed.

With alternating rhymes, we were reciting a poem again, except this one would be written on the pages of our feet and recorded in the Book of Pain.

CHAPTER 8: CAROL

"I CAN CONSUME ANYTHING and everything you can feed me." Spector adjusted himself and rubbed his hands together to signal an appetite. It sounded like sandpaper working against the grain to me. I continued with my story to avoid the trap of observing him in greater detail.

"Well, when I found out about Paul's kidnapping, I couldn't pinpoint an emotion. I mean, I felt empty or hollow inside, like someone had reached in and stolen my baby as well."

The keyboard clicked rapidly. The ghostwriter's eyes went cross-eyed and his head bowed to me like the figure of the crucified Christ on the mantle. I could see a bald spot swirling like a twister on his head. On top of all the damage his body had endured, his hair had also decided to jump ship in patches, as if purposely trying to insult the injury more. Broken had graduated to shattered on his body now, and soon the rest of the pieces would float away too.

"Tessa has been sick for days. She refuses to eat."

I pointed to my dog. I needed to change the subject before he noticed my intense observation of his flaws and injuries. I don't know why they intrigued me. In the past, I was never one to enjoy a train wreck. And here I was, slowing down traffic just to get a closer glimpse of his battle scars. Not as interested as I was in this mutant of a man, Tessa waited at the window as if expecting Paul to fly back home. She waited in the same spot, even though, just the other day, a bird had crashed into the glass, entranced by its own reflection, or fooled by the refraction of the sun. Spector had pouted when I digressed to pity it, as if it was an annoying triviality. For some unorthodox reason, I imagined him naked in that instant. Surgery scars decorating the skin on his torso. A shrivelled-up penis, hairless legs, and toes without nails.

"Continue."

Apparently, he had repeated this command a number of times. He might have seen through to my imaginings, I worried, which would give him the upper hand. I felt the need to retaliate with my own surge of emotion. At the very least, it might shock him into a new reaction.

"Then I started to hate Paul violently."

Spector raised his head now, in slow motion. He stopped typing.

"You were angry, Mrs. Shell?"

"No, I hated Paul enough to kill him for leaving me. He left me for a story, for God's sake."

"Mrs. Shell, with all due respect, I can't write that down."

"Why?"

He took a sip of his alcohol, tempered by a dash of coffee. He didn't even wince after swallowing. His sensory taste had deserted him.

"Well, I am trying to portray you as a victim, Mrs. Shell, not a vengeful wife."

"Yes?"

"Victims are not usually filled with hate, Mrs. Shell, or malice for that matter."

"Are you sure about that?"

He offered me his impatience by gesturing with his hand to stop speaking. His closed eyes communicated disapproval or perhaps disgust with me. The more I wanted to talk about this, the more he tried to settle me down with hand gestures.

"So what do *you* want to 'portray' me as, Mr. Ghostman?"

"As *'the cut worm forgives the plough.'*"

I had heard that line before, but couldn't remember where and when. Had Paul read it to me during one of our menial arguments? We had collaborated on so many, usually related to his work, his time, his absences, my loneliness, and my neglected needs.

"Mrs. Shell?"

"Sorry. You're right, Mr. Spector. I'm deeply in love with my husband."

The keyboard found a running start again. Nonetheless, I wondered what he wrote behind the screen. When I stopped narrating, I expected him to stop writing, yet he persisted in my silent moments. An awkward game of Battleship, no doubt, and he had already sunk a few of my boats. Often, he would look up to inspect me while his fingers danced on the keys like feet tapping or legs flailing about, almost separate from my control of them.

He finally noticed that I noticed.

"Sorry. Let me explain. I am painting you with language. That's how you have to see it. You are speaking, and I am recording your words. However, you are also posing for me, sometimes in the nude," he said, laughing. "Metaphorically speaking, of course."

Although his explanation should have insulted me, it flattered me instead. That he also imagined me naked, posing for him like a model.

He was painting me with language. At once, I felt like I didn't need to speak anymore. He could read and write me at the same time. He studied my body language, as I did his, except he created a better version of me, while I feared a more disturbing one of him. Best of all, his intentions spoke volumes. He recreated me with words to impress the public's eye. To create a masterpiece for them to remember. Iconic.

It appeased me, so I continued with what I felt he wanted to hear, with what I imagined myself experiencing in my most romantic dreams.

"Paul and I met at a sugar bush."

He grunted and nodded.

"I was a teacher once, elementary school. Private, of course; actually, don't write that down. We were on a field trip. He was a young local reporter then, and he was doing a story on the technology of tree tapping. I remember that day. We instructed the kids to hold onto a single rope so as not to lose one and they became entangled in the sap wires. It was a big mess, and Paul and his cameraman offered their help. We couldn't stop laughing. There was a strong scent of smoke in the forest, I remember, combined with a steel tub of water boiling over a fire. The sugar in the air made it sparkle. And then we ate pancakes. That was our first real date. Pancakes with real maple syrup, and I loved every minute of it."

I finished the story and he persisted in his typing, transcribing my layered image through the new palette of language I gave him. I leaned back. Tessa lay there with her chin on the floor, whining with glistening eyes, crystallized tears on her snout, now grey and dry. She hadn't eaten for days and was sick to her stomach. I watched her while the ghostwriter spun his fiction, wondering why I hadn't felt the same aversion to food. I was hungry as hell.

CHAPTER 9: LEA

"THEY MAKE ME FEEL BETTER," Paul said.

"What?"

"The Proverbs from the poem."

I laid on my side with the tail of my back against the wall. My feet bled into the spaces between my toes. The second onslaught of torture had surpassed the first in severity. They had set my body on fire, and it burned beneath my skin every-where. I assumed Paul felt the same way. He didn't moan in the aftermath this time. I could hear his voice in the dark from across the room requesting more poetry from "The Marriage of Heaven and Hell."

They had whipped the bottoms of my feet first. He had watched with interest as I writhed and screamed on the floor. He studied me in the light this time, like he had found a trigger in me, or a secret to the suffering that he wanted to keep to himself. He understood something more than just the pain. He had seen me in time, in the history of my screams. And I had heard myself in this history as a young girl touching the heated coil on the stove for the first time, or as the adolescent who wanted it to end when Dave Marcini took advantage of me for the first time and it hurt for days. I had let those ancestral sufferings out of me, and he had seen them for what they were—scabs accidentally loosened.

"Please. For some reason, it makes me forget my feet," Paul begged.

"'The pride of the peacock is the glory of God.
The lust of the goat is the bounty of God.
The wrath of the lion is the wisdom of God.'"

He interrupted me to offer a proverb himself. *"'The naked-*
ness of woman is the work of God.'"

I stopped. I could hear him anticipating more with slight
movement, but I was growing tired of his impatience with me,
his insistence on my service as a poetic nurse.

To escape this duty, I wondered if anyone else had seen the
films our torturers recorded of us. Why were they taking so
many pictures? And why did the old man in the scarf sketch
the scenes? He didn't seem to flinch as he depicted our pain
with a pencil. What were they attempting to create, a picture
book of our suffering? Or were they recording our suffering
for masochistic reasons? There seemed to be a hidden artistic
motive in their designs, like they were conducting research on
our pain tolerance, or possibly, the strength of our spirits. I
felt embarrassed to have screamed so recklessly, so wildly, yet
I felt stronger when I recovered my breath. The fire of my pain
had cauterized something within me and the ashes fertilized
newer, cleaner avenues of thought and perception.

"Are you embarrassed by the pain?" I asked him.

"Only when you hear me."

"I try not to."

"Me too. I can't help myself."

There was a pause. My feet throbbed to steal what little
oxygen remained in the room for healing. I could feel deep
grooves in the skin now scabbing with blood, tightening the
nerves in my soles.

"You enjoyed it," I said, calling him out.

"Yes, I did."

"I was screaming, and they were whipping my feet, and you
didn't want them to stop."

"I was sorry they did," Paul said.

A dripping silence occupied the room now. It puddled in the space between us, invisible.

"But you didn't want me to die, Paul."

"No, on the contrary. I wanted you to live."

"Live enough to suffer their torture."

"Yes."

"Were you thinking they would tire from their efforts?"

"Yes."

"Did you want me to suffer more, Paul?"

"Yes, but not anymore."

"Why?"

"Because I don't love myself anymore," Paul said like a confession. "I can't love at all. I never could, not even my...."

I imagined a world of water between us now. It was black and salted and life refused to exist below its surface. Yet, it was warm and sticky like tar, healing in some way.

"*'The cistern contain: the fountain overflows,'*" I recited the poem again. It was a constant now, the poem, a blanket to warm us both.

"*'One thought fills immensity,'*" he said.

CHAPTER 10: CAROL

SPECTOR STOPPED WRITING. "What? What is it?" I was growing impatient with these recent stalls.

"Nothing. I can't make anything of this information, Mrs. Shell. We're going to have to start again."

I rose from my chair. Timothy sat in on this session, his cellphone vibrating every two minutes. The buzzing sound invited radioactivity into my womb, while the signal forced Timothy to lift his heavy body from the wooden chair causing it to creak. Other squeaking noises followed as he stomped over loose boards in the hardwood floors. They were supposed to be immovable.

"This is my life. This is how I grew up," I answered the ghostwriter.

"It's too ... protected."

"My parents were well off. They made sure to take care of me."

"I realize that, Mrs. Shell. However, the readers who will buy your book will be looking for an angle to empathize with."

In-between calls, Timothy glanced up from his phone, as if sensing conflict in the disagreement.

"We all want security, but we don't empathize with it. You need to live a life of conflict to tell a story," Mr. Spector argued.

"It isn't enough that I'm pregnant and my husband has been kidnapped and tortured?"

"No, it isn't. That could happen to anyone. You need to be

anyone, but somebody special at the same time, Mrs. Shell."

Timothy's heavy metal ring tone, signifying a call from a specific colleague, broke the silence again and he returned to his unheard partner. He attacked the caller with a barrage of agent logic. "I told you, we want to saturate the daytime market before we move to prime time. Daytime is when we can maximize the single mother/neglected wife demographic that will boost us when we move to the prime-time war-related news shows. You know what I mean? The family structure is there already, so we just have to make it work for us."

Although I had fed the dog already, I made my way to the cupboard where I kept Tessa's treats. I dropped one in front of the dog's nose, and Tessa took it in her mouth. She placed it delicately on the rising pile of her food dish. She had become a Gandhi dog, and her protest continued as those around her resorted to the most violent means available in civilized society.

I picked up a book from the shelf to distract myself from the dog and the ghostwriter's hideous visage. If only he wasn't so omniscient. With those sunken eye sockets, he haunted me at night with questions in my sleep and how I should answer them. He was the embodiment of emptiness, staring at me and digging into my soul for my story until, when it was dug out, I felt as empty as he looked. And now I had told him everything, and it was still not enough to satisfy his fictional appetite.

When Timothy finally pressed the red button on the phone, he approached me at the bookshelf. He stood right behind me again, upright. I could feel his belt buckle on the curve of my buttocks.

"Do you realize, from behind, you don't even look pregnant?"

I didn't answer him. I smiled to myself nonetheless. The timing of his words was impeccable. He could save me with one word, I thought, because I waited on him to speak to me. His words were so precise and accurate to my needs that I couldn't help myself from comparing them to Paul's silence when he returned home, or the fake, repetitive catchphrases he used on television.

I pulled a book from the shelf, a favourite of Paul's. I stared at the pictures and ignored the words, hoping Timothy would fill them in himself. "What is it, Carol?" he whispered.

I turned around with a subtle step backwards to put some polite distance between us. "My life is of no interest."

"Your life is everyone's interest."

"Tell him, then."

Timothy glanced at Conrad Spector. The ghostwriter rubbed the back of his head as he reviewed his last written segment.

"Do you want me to hire someone else, Carol?"

"Is it me?"

"That's what we want. You and only you."

Spector dismissed himself with a polite wave and exited to the tiny balcony outside. He would often return smelling of smoke and pollution. Rather rudely, I must say, he wouldn't turn off the laptop before he left. When I placed my hands on the table, I could feel the warmth from its radiating battery. One previous day, when we had encountered a similar road block, I'd wanted to push him over the edge of the balcony. He made me feel fat and bloated and privileged and useless.

"Listen, Carol. You don't have to tell everything as it was," said Timothy. "What you remember is far less interesting than what you want to remember, or hope to remember. The story lies in how you feel now and how you see everything back then from the point of view you have now. That's the truest way to tell a story."

He extended his hand to a view of the city from the curtain window wall. It was smoggy today. The ghostwriter seemed to be inhaling it as cigarette smoke released from his nostrils. He butted out, and Timothy offered some last words of encouragement.

"He doesn't know anything about you except what you want to tell him. You have the power. He is just a middleman."

Spector took his place at the table again. I joined him soon after and so did Timothy, who sat across from me. Supportive. Ready to listen. Interested in what I had to say. He laid his phone on the table and with a theatrical gesture, his arm arching up and diving straight down with his index finger extended, he pressed the red button to turn it off.

I made a decision then and there. I would rewrite my life the way I would want it to be read. The ghost would transcribe from my very tongue. I would treat him like the ghost he was, insignificant to my created reality.

"Okay," I began, before pausing to think some more about it.

"I was sexually assaulted as a young girl, but I never told anyone. I was too afraid. Not even my parents or my friends … not even my husband knows. But it devastated me, and I have never been able to fully recover until now. What happened to my husband awoke this repressed memory in me." I spoke quickly and without emotion.

Spector smiled. He paused a moment to think it over himself. There were so many possibilities now. Timothy nudged him.

"Let's go. Get these notes down. The woman has a story to tell."

Mr. Spector buried his head into the keyboard, and Timothy turned to me. A smile for support, a smirk for respect. It was somewhere in-between.

CHAPTER 11: LEA

IN THE MIDDLE OF THE DAY OR NIGHT, a chorus of footsteps raided the torture room to wrap our naked bodies in cloth as if we were mummies in Ancient Egypt. When they wrapped me in this tight cocoon, I tasted herbs. Hallucinogenic. Intoxicating. Poisonous. I couldn't tell, but they salted my broken lips.

After a prolonged silence, hard pieces of wood cracked on my knees and elbows. Paul rolled about in the dark as well. He banged into the wall. They hit him with sticks, too. When I lost my breath and coughed into myself, my body must have convulsed in panic because the assault stopped instantly. I listened to a chain dragging across the floor and latching onto another link pressing into the top of my head. They dragged me by this steel chain to a warmer room. The beatings continued along the way. One struck my burned shoulder. I screamed, and the high pitch of my voice nearly tore the wrap. At least, I imagined it that way. Through the folds of cloth, it must have sounded like a groan to them.

Eventually, a knife cut through the cloth some time later, slicing my arm by accident. The blood dripped in a line to my palm. My hands were freed from the wrapping and buckled together with chains behind my back. My feet were similarly shackled. They waited for quite some time with my hair in a fisted grasp, before they revealed my face to a bright light. When they removed the head wrap completely, a spotlight shone down on me like The Annunciation. Paul sat next to me, spitting blood onto the cloth. He moaned and spat until a man clobbered him on the head to soften his complaints to a whimper.

The preparatory abuse halted at the squeaking sound of approaching wheels. The spotlights dimmed. I saw a computer screen before us. The young boy with the long eyelashes, a scarf nearly falling below his chin, pushed it by on a dolly so close that it nearly flattened Paul's face.

"Who is this?"

Paul squinted. Another man to the side of the computer screen, covered in a scarf, pointed to highlighted words on the screen. Paul refused to answer.

"Who is this?" The man asked again.

Paul turned his head away. Two men from behind him struck at his temples with open palms. His face smashed into the screen, threatening to shatter it like a mirror. They pulled his hair so that his eyes would face the screen again. The hair tore out. It didn't faze Paul; his tolerance to pain had graduated to beyond mere hair-pulling. One of the men dropped his stick and jerked Paul's head into position.

"What is this name?" The man pointed again.

"I don't know," Paul finally said. The group attacked him. While they did so, the young boy gently moved the computer screen to me. Behind his loose mask, his almond -shaped eyes revealed friendship, expectation.

"Can you please tell us who this is? This person is interfering with our mission."

I recognized the name of the search engine. I had used it before. The young boy pointed to a list entitled, "Hottest Searches."

From behind, a man tried to pull my hair but it was too short to grasp at my neck, so he pinched me by the ear. His fingers were rough-skinned and thick. Strong.

"Who is this name?" He repeated to me.

I mouthed the name at the top of the list. It read, "Carol Shell." Below it read the headline, "Journalists Kidnapped."

Their apparent mission had placed second to Paul's wife. They must have known who she was. What did they want from Paul? A confession?

"Don't tell them." Paul spoke through bloodied teeth. The men took a break to catch their breaths while the young technician positioned an Internet camera on the desk, next to the screen. I looked behind me to see knives hanging on the wall. They appeared to be hung as decoration only. My stepfather had hung two swords with similar red velvet handles above our fireplace in Toronto. He had crossed them for decoration's sake. I once removed the sword from the casing and it wasn't sharp. For the precocious nature of my curiosity, I received a beating from him.

A man with a dark grey scarf turned the computer screen around while the boy typed. Another held the round eye above the screen. Yet another took his place to the left to hold up cue cards. They would not record this interview with the video camera. They were going to stream this video right away on the Internet. A knee nudged me from behind to read the cue cards.

"Save us. Please. They are torturing us," I read out loud in a monotone voice.

The knee nudged me again.

"They will kill one of us soon and break the medium of communication between our worlds if you don't meet their demands."

The man holding the camera eye lowered it to show Paul's bloody face. The knee nudged me to continue.

"That is Paul Shell."

The camera eye lifted. The man walked it over to the knives hanging on the wall.

"They will cut our heads off and silence all voices of the medium," I read. The man dropped the camera eye. Paul and I were dragged again to the basement room. Our faces were once again covered. This time around they strapped us to the wall. Paul tried to breathe through the cloth but found it difficult to do so. He choked on something, like his own tongue. In-between his coughs, I heard a blowing, hissing sound enter the room. I could feel a familiar warmth approaching my naked body from behind again. The distorted blowing sharpened to a harsher hissing. The young boy stumbled into my peripheral line of vision. He held the hissing tool, which shook, in his thin hands. His face above the scarf perspired noticeably, and drops clung for life on his long eyelashes. He looked as if he wanted to cry, fearful with this foreign weapon in his hand not attached to his computer screen or linked to a camera.

He had never trained or studied the use of analog tools. His older superiors now tortured him in another way, initiating him into their circle of pain, making him into a man, as they would say back home. I braced myself as they pushed him closer to me, and more than fear I felt empathy for the young boy. This time there would be no burning with an iron. This time the fire became real and sharp as a knife in his trembling hand. The sharpened edge of the blowtorch engraved my flesh and threatened to push into the tip of my spine. Before I fainted, I thought I heard him speak in English.

"I'm sorry."

CHAPTER 12: **CAROL**

"THE LIFE OF A WAR JOURNALIST'S WIFE is a real life of terror." No longer did it satisfy me to simply spill out my story to Conrad Spector. I had adjusted the tone of voice to imply dictation, just as Timothy advised me.

"It involves an acceptance of situations and an appreciation for self-sacrifice. Up until this moment, I was more than prepared to sacrifice myself for my husband's aspirations. But as a mother, I cannot sacrifice my baby. My baby is everything to me. My baby hasn't even met the first man in her life. And he has already betrayed her in some way. This is why I have to believe he will return to save her from his own absence in her life. He has to return. I am prepared to sacrifice more of myself to bring him back, even if it means I am not seen as myself anymore, but only as the journalist's wife who wants her husband to be in the waiting room to see his child being born."

Spector glanced upwards as if to expect the sincerity of tears after this admission, but I felt more sinister for creating it. I envisioned myself dropping these empathetic, literary bombshells onto a gullible public. The private show pleased him. We sat in a café in Greenwich Village. Timothy had suggested I make myself available in a more eclectic environment. He didn't want people to see me as an elitist holed up in her fancy condominium. If I were to become everywoman, I had to associate with everywoman. That was the marketing game plan, which required, amongst other details, an entirely new wardrobe. An assortment of casual clothes and jeans and punky T-shirts would make me more appealing to the young adult, new adult generation.

This was the generation with "energy," explained Timothy, "and misguided energy is always looking for a human leader."

He was right. Everyone recognized me in the Village. Some had approached the table asking for autographs and phone pictures, while others, very kindly, offered me words of reassurance in passing.

"We are praying for your husband, Mrs. Shell."

"You are a brave woman, Mrs. Shell."

"You should write a book, Mrs. Shell. My boyfriend hasn't been captured by terrorists," said one woman, who chuckled nervously. "But he always works late hours. I know how you feel."

"Your baby will see her father one day, don't you worry, Ma'am."

I smiled and dismissed all of them with a motherly pose of approval and grace, although they weren't much younger than me. This was another detail Timothy suggested. "Act your age," he said, "and don't let your name age you. But at the same time, remember: the mother angle is your trump card. That's your mainstay, and whenever you take a picture, draw attention to that gold mine of a tummy."

Following his advice, I often posed in my mirror at home to perfect my stance. I slanted my head to the left and nodded at the same time, my hair delicately swept to my shoulder. Spector interrupted.

"What about your own dreams and aspirations, Mrs. Shell? I'm sure your audience would love to hear what you plan to do next, especially if, you know, he dies, of course."

"If he *dies*?"

"Yes, Mrs. Shell. And before you start, remember, helplessness and desperation are two valuable angles for any work of literature. A reader loves to follow a protagonist who is liable to be pitied. We all want to feel sorry for someone, and if possible, righteously indignant. It drives us to want to learn more about them. We want to devour that moment of climactic *denouement*, then let it ride down a hill and past the point of no return, before we reach a profitable resolution."

"Very well then. I want to start a psychiatric care foundation for wives and girlfriends of soldiers who are lost at war."

"Perfect." Spector digested it with his fingers. He hummed as he ate my words, savouring every bit of their sweet and salty flavor.

"After they place the flag on that coffin, everyone makes their way to the next widow in line. They walk away and forget the poor woman who has to find a place for that flag in her home. Does she keep it folded in a cupboard somewhere? Does she take it out when her children are old enough? Or does she bury it somewhere in a box because it is too painful to see the cause that eclipsed the love and commitment of her loved one?"

"Beautiful, Carol. Keep it coming."

Carol? He had never called me Carol before. Was my story making us intimate, too close for comfort? It didn't matter now. His *created* Carol could feel her body exhaling chemicals with every word. And this new literary vision now detoxified the pollutants of worry, regret, and guilt collecting within me. I felt I could have talked for hours about my dreams, if it meant polishing the varnish of my newfound celebrity. I felt like I could have gone on to say that I considered other men in my life. Wealthy men with little ambition but to pamper me. Royalty, perhaps, from monarchs of distant lands, wishing to place my image on their currency.

I remembered a series of lines from a Shakespearean play, one Paul once quoted to open a segment on his interview with the president: "Some are born great.... Some achieve greatness.... And some have greatness thrust upon them." The words rang true for me now. I felt like my suffering or what suffering I was supposed to be enduring found an oasis of hope and fulfillment in the possibilities of a new future, one where my baby would nearly forget about the man who died for a cause once it lost relevance with the next day's news.

"Most of all, I want my husband to be a part of everything I do. He is inside of me. I can feel him kicking through his baby's feet. If I end up widowed, I will make sure no woman will feel alone because of a war in a distant land. I will make a Heaven out of their Hell."

Spector struck the keyboard with a sharp snap of his finger. "I think it's time for another coffee," he deemed.

"Do we have enough, Mr. Spector?"

"Enough for me to piece together for the auction tomorrow. That's for sure. And definitely enough to promote your publicity tour next week. Let's just hope they don't kill him before then."

He laughed to himself, not realizing the rudeness of his words, while he perused the coffee menu.

I thought the same possibility quite some time ago, but now it didn't move me to react as much.

CHAPTER 13: LEA

I CLOSELY WATCHED A NEW FIGURE enter the torture room. This one walked like a woman, on her toes, with narrow feet sliding close to one another, pointed inwards. She was clothed in a brown robe, with a monk's hood. Barefoot, she paced about the room nodding and speaking to herself in a foreign language. I looked over to Paul to see if he noticed her. He was lying on his back, staring up at the black ceiling. He might have been dead. From my vantage point, I couldn't tell. The woman in the Franciscan frock might have come to take his spirit away, or mine, though she possessed no scythe in sight. She didn't speak to either of us. I couldn't see her face. This vision of her distracted me from the fire-burrowed holes on my back and arms.

"Hello?" I said, testing her.

The figure turned away to a corner of the room, where our torturers often left us water. A knotted rope held her waist together. "Can you hear me?" I asked.

No answer.

"Paul?"

No answer.

"Paul?"

No answer.

I crawled over to the bare feet under the monk's habit. I wanted to touch them. The figure sensed my proximity and moved away to another corner. The white rope of her belt lit the area where she stood. I couldn't see her hands or smell her breath in the room.

I found myself by the book and the piece of carpet and the plate of flat bread. The carpet was rough to my touch and the book soft but thick in pages, and I couldn't smell the bread. Scentless bread, devoid of sustenance.

"Paul?"

"Leave me alone. I want to die."

His tone preached anger again. The blowtorch had inspired a new fury in him. Its unexpected method had insulted his fears, for he now knew he wasn't creative enough to anticipate the horrors of future visits. I had never felt such pain before either, and yet I felt more alive for it. I had been reborn in the pain. In the midst of it all, I had felt candles lit in parts of my body and soul that I had presumed dead. My eyes didn't hurt. They weren't strained anymore, and my mind floated in the liquid of my skull. It didn't stick to the walls or try to press its way out at my temples or at the bridge of my nose. My mind felt empowered by the torture, ironically, assigning my senses heightened abilities, like seeing beyond the dark walls of this prison and out onto a longer, wheat-waving landscape. In my mind's eye, I walked through the sheaths, separating a path for myself, encountering people I had deemed forgotten to me in the museum of my regrets. They offered me forgiving smiles: my daughter-to-be, my former husband, my deceased father. Their embraces welcomed me like a brisk breeze. Such escaping imaginations made me crave the blowtorch again in the same way my blood boiled for the cooling sedation of narcotics.

"Why are you here?" I asked the figure. "Where are you from?"

"I told you to leave me alone," repeated Paul. He writhed on the floor. His back creaked every time he moved or spoke, as if his rusted scabs needed oil.

The figure turned her back on me. On hands and knees, I

followed her to the padlocked door. Paul started to beg again. "Please. More poetry, Lea."

"You remember it as well as I do, recite it to yourself."

"I need to listen to it. I can't hear it the same way if I speak." His voice soon withered away into sinus snores.

I pressed my lips to the door as if to speak to the figure who had managed in the darkness to disappear to the other side. I remembered other women like her, in similar uniform, inviting me to the convent after my father died and my mother was hospitalized. It was quiet and dark. A sister approached me with a rough hand. With her fingertips, she felt how soft my hands were. How young and pink.

"Lea. You have disobeyed. Don't you realize that to create this little flower is the labour of ages? We would like you to join us, but you have yet to understand the mysteries of the rosary."

In this memory, I could feel the beads of the rosary scratching my neck. They forced me to listen to the words in the book by sticking it in my face.

"He has called you to suffer like the little flower in the storm, but you have failed to answer Him."

She pulled my hand across the kneeler. I remembered that the kneeler had a red velvet cushion for the knees. The nuns kept it in the sacristy, the room where we were taught to adore the Host. When I extended my hand, the sister struck it with a belt. I remembered a child version of myself holding in the tears, trying to endure more. The Sister struck me until spit bubbled from my mouth and spilled onto my uniform. I was sent to pray before the Host, but I was too angry to address Him. Too upset to be called.

"You never know what enough is unless you know what is more than enough," I repeated to myself at the end of this memory, recalling how the nuns described devotion. I hadn't realized that Paul could hear me. He was awake in his sleep, more frustrated than ever with me.

"I can't hear you. Speak to my sores, please. The words fill the sores."

"*You never know what enough is unless you know what is more than enough,*" I repeated, picking myself up from the ground. I walked over to him. I could feel him scrambling to the wall by instinct. He couldn't see me, but I could hear him sucking in wind from his mouth. I couldn't sit on the other side of the room anymore. I dropped down to his shivering body. It rattled against its bones.

"No, please don't touch me," he begged.

"I was lost, and now I am found. I was dead, and now I am alive," I said to him.

"That's not from the poem," he said, refuting me.

I pushed his body down and ran my hand softly down his welted skin.

"I have a wife. I have a wife and a child."

For the first time in so many years, I needed to love someone, even if I knew he didn't love me in return.

CHAPTER 14: CAROL

I IMAGINED THE COLOUR-DRAINED FACE of a man in the painting as my husband suffering in a black room. The man's hands seemed to pull his flesh downwards until the palette is mixed into a chaotic undertow of dark shades and scratched layers. It was a popular painting in the ritzy New York art gallery. Other needle-nosed connoisseurs behind me breathed over my shoulder in an attempt to persuade me to move. From behind, I suspected, they couldn't tell I was pregnant, or else they might have shown better manners, or at the very least, employed the use of gum. Perhaps I had spent too long in front of this particular painting, projecting my personal interpretation upon it. I felt uncomfortable and naïve to the virtues of art-viewing etiquette.

Many of these war-inspired images shook me with a karmic sickness. The baby in my womb pressed against my ribs in discomfort. I moved on to the next painting in the lined sequence on the wall. Other admirers at the gallery auction for fallen soldiers' wives mingled with champagne glasses filled with blood-coloured wine. Timothy was somewhere, on his phone presumably. I was the guest of honour. The artist himself floated from painting to painting in the spirit of a condolence telegram.

The next painting across the hall settled my nervous rumblings a bit. I was looking at the backside of a naked woman sprawled out in a green bush, hovering over a naked baby. To the left of the woman, a man, who was partially submerged in the green, exulted with his hands in the air. An aureole of hair, possibly sunrays, framed his blurred, devilish visage. Suddenly, I felt aroused by him. I wasn't sure if it was the portrait itself or the hormones fluctuating within me, but I was dripping, and not because my water broke. I worried, as I once did in the GNN studio, if a streak of it would line my freshly shaved leg to the stiletto heel. Closing my eyes, I tried to convince myself to cool down and not to flush in the face, or else someone like Timothy might smell my heat or misinterpret its message. I pressed my legs together, the moisture absorbing into my panties. The more I tried, the more I saw Timothy in my thoughts, pressing into me from behind.

"Are you ready to speak, Carol?"

Timothy had snuck up on me again, startling me. For some reason, I could never hear his footsteps. I placed a hand over my mouth, before composing myself by fanning the program before my face.

"Is the press here yet, Timothy?"

"Yes. They want to meet you first. Are you all right? You seem a little flushed."

"Yes, I'm fine. Any television coverage?" I asked.

"Of course, some of the local New York networks, but this is just a step forward to national coverage. Lots of influential people here. Some politicians. A few celebrities, and some editors and critics. It would do well to speak to them. Good coverage can help with the promotion of the book."

I nodded while perusing the swanky crowd. The buzzing sound of oscillating voices intermingled with the *click-clack* of high heels tap dancing against the cement floor. The noise lowered in volume once I appeared behind a dais. The artist of the paintings joined me with a proud smile, and we took some photos together. His name was Marseau. Cameras flashed in my eye before the deafening silence of the gallery forced me to speak. I saw a young blonde girl near the back of the room. She was the only one in the crowd not listening to me. She was staring at the portrait of the devil ... the one that disturbed me into arousal.

I chose a blunt approach with my opening address. "I wish I knew more about art. I only see what I feel these days."

Patches of red bloomed on cheeks in the crowd. Their eyes glistened into gloss. My voice felt empowered by their attention. They waited for my next word with sincere attention, all except for the young girl at the back. She slid from painting to painting, as if not hearing me. I considered her rude, but I envied her ability to close out everything. Despite my newfound fame, I remembered the privacy of being a nobody. It had its advantages, of course, like not being recognized by excited strangers. Not having to perfect my makeup before I exited the condominium building. The worry of paparazzi.

They waited for me to speak again.

"But I also realize how important it is to see the war through Marseau's lens. I watch the news every evening hoping to see my husband rescued by American soldiers and walking to a plane that could bring him home. And when I don't, I bury those strong emotions within me. Which is why, I have written a book about the torture of not knowing what will happen next. It's not easy to live with, but I know many wives of soldiers are dealing with the same horrors."

A loud clap incited a host of others. It soon turned into an excited ovation. A man in uniform removed a handkerchief to dab at a tear, so I blew him a kiss and mouthed the word "Thank you."

Behind the man in uniform, Timothy watched with a subtle thumbs-up. He was proud of me, of my ability to provoke emotion with simple white lies. I was proud of myself, I suppose. I had learned that you could change people with words. It didn't take much. Just some context and timing, with a little pretended honesty. As Timothy once noted to me, "Dumb people are so easily swayed by the prospect of belief. Give them something pure to believe in and they will surely follow."

The young girl at the back of the gallery stopped and turned to face me for a second, awakened by the applause. As if disgusted by it, she left through the side door. I could see her skipping freely through the window, blending into another light.

CHAPTER 15: A WINTER PARTY

"WHY DID YOU DO THAT TO ME?" Paul asked, spitting on himself by accident.

I refused to answer him. I was satisfied enough with having sinned in my heart. It was something more to torture myself with. Committing an adulterous act with a married man, who whispered softly for me to stop before he let his body melt in my mouth. I had become the blowtorch, my mouth hissing, sharpening, and then burning what was burning inside of him.

"Do you believe you are suffering for her? Or your unborn child?"

He remained silent. I was reading his mind, and he knew I was capable to see more into his guilt.

"Danger will not avoid them because these men burned you with a torch and iron. You are in Hell, Paul. You are suffering for the dead. For people like me."

"Then who are you suffering for?" he asked me. He rolled over so as not to face me. His voice reverberated off the wall.

"For those who raped me. For the boy who held a torch to my back. For those who enjoy inflicting pain."

"Like yourself."

"Yes. For me above everyone else."

"Is it possible to live and suffer for the same cause?" he asked.

"If that cause is freedom."

"We are not free."

"I have never been more free."

He stood up and before me, now, naked. He had lost a lot of weight and his hip bones were as sharp as knives. It was one of the first times he had risen to the standing position. My intimate touch, and maybe some of the stale bread we were finally digesting, may have invigorated him. He walked to the centre of the room and grabbed the chain hanging there. He had something to explain. "For years, in my church, I attended knowing I never wanted to go. You know when you do something solely because you believe you are supposed to be there?"

I understood exactly what he meant. Playing the part meant denying yourself for the sake of saving face or forcing guilt-driven belief.

"I would find myself just staring at the cross over the altar," he said. "It was just an ornament to me. No symbol of worship. Every time I saw it, I prayed before it with an empty heart. I mean, I recognized poetry in his stretched limbs and respected the metaphorical royalty in a crown of thorns. Sometimes, I even marvelled at the beauty of his sunken ribs and wondered whether one nail held his two feet together. But I couldn't feel anything more sincere. I couldn't feel his suffering. I couldn't feel the pain."

He pulled the cross on his chain before his eyes so he could see it more clearly in the dark.

"And so, I lost myself in the ritual of hiding. At the back of the church. In a group of people. At a charity event. Pennies in a cup as I walked by the same homeless man on my way to work. I feared being caught not rising above myself."

He had finally come out of his phony shell, and I admired the tone of his voice. He wasn't speaking to a camera now or *for* one. Our suffering had been consummated and now we were sharing in the aftermath.

I joined him in the moment. "I made myself deaf too, Paul. For years, I could feel and hear whispers. Calling me to something. I have heard them since I was a little girl."

He turned to me and listened.

"Since my father died, I made myself hate everything or everyone sent to love me in return. I wanted to suffer above all else because I have never seen meaning in anything else."

"*Improvement makes straight roads; but the crooked roads without Improvement, are roads to Genius,*" Paul said, reciting the poem again as if to find a connection with my own words.

"Precisely." I felt a new pain in my chest, a splitting apart of something. I pressed my hand against the burns on my shoulders. The muscles were pliant enough for me to feel the bumpy landscape of bone.

When I sighed, it provoked something in him, and he ran over to me and placed his hands around my neck. He squeezed, and I could see his eyes turn red. He was impatient with the slow turn of the torture room screw, and he wanted to take it as far as he could in that instant. He was going to surprise our captors with the corpse of a woman who barely reacted to their tortures, and then laugh in their faces for having missed their own opportunity. Then he was going to hide it all behind the dead bodies of withdrawal, torture, and poetry.

"*Sooner murder an infant in its cradle than nurse unacted desires*'" he said, squeezing and squeezing, as if provoked by the words.

"*Sooner murder an infant in its cradle than nurse unacted desires.*'" It was all he had to say.

"*Enough! Or too much!*'" I whispered, struggling to answer him. He let go of my neck. When he removed his hands, he could not straighten his fingers. They were claw-shaped and arthritic, just like mine. We were transforming into the brutality of our sufferings and defining ourselves in accordance.

He made his way to the wall and slunk to the sitting position. There he cried into his claws, trying to melt them into hands again with his breath.

CHAPTER 16: CAROL

I FELL IN AND OUT OF SLEEP on the couch, waiting for Timothy's call. I placed the cellphone he bought for me on the table nearby. He programmed a dial tone specific to his own calls. I was hesitant to accept the gift, but he stressed the importance of having a lifeline on me at all times. He also purchased a case for the phone designed to block radiation. He said I could clip it on to my purse. Suede and fashionable, I wondered how much blocking it really did.

Perhaps the auction for my book had failed to attract a buyer. Maybe they didn't believe my story and all of the fabrications. Many, after I reviewed them with the ghostwriter, seemed melodramatic to me in retrospect. Like a soap opera inspired by the steroid of insecurity.

I pulled the cellphone closer to me and flipped it open. Timothy used the phone to take a picture of me at the art gallery night. He found the best angle of my face and I appreciated how he saw me through his own lens. He always found the most seductive point of view. He programmed his number and that of my obstetrician in the contacts folder. This surprised me, although I appreciated having someone thinking for me, serving my needs. It helped me to focus on making up stories. We needed to get the book out so that they could rush its publication. Timothy wanted it in print in time to promote it fully on the daytime show I have always dreamed of guesting on since I was a little girl.

The pink phone failed to show any missed calls. Close to one in the morning, and I started to get a little anxious. He wouldn't want to wake me, perhaps. He was always so thoughtful that way. But if it was good news, wouldn't he want to share it with me right away? Or would he defer to the morning, to share it over breakfast? I wasn't sure what to expect from him, and maybe that was the core of his appeal—unpredictability. It fuelled his charisma and confidence. It furthered trust and belief in him. And yet, he did promise that at the very least, he would call me with the amount of the sale, no matter how late the auction finished.

A soft knock sounded on the door. Tessa didn't bother barking at the visitor at this hour. She slept, half-dead on the carpet next to the food dish she refused to eat from. She made herself more than sick. She was cancerous with grief, as if expecting her internal clock to force the dying process.

Anticipating Timothy at the door, I adjusted myself in the mirror before opening it. I was a little apprehensive that he would see me in my thinner nightie wear, and without make-up, but for some reason, I believed he had already seen me exposed from the inside out. I opened the door only to find the disappointing image of the ghostwriter leaning against the door frame. Conrad Spector was dressed like a young man this late evening, without his tie and vest, sporting a raggedy baseball cap. In his hands, he held wilting red carnations. I could see a $2.99 price sticker holding them together in a bouquet. In his other hand, he held a bottle of wine and a paper bag.

"I thought we should celebrate."

He lifted the gifts for me to see. I had never seen a ghost smile before, and on his face, the opening revealed some dead, blackened teeth.

"It's late," I said.

"I know. I just received the news from the publisher. The book sold. Timothy hasn't called you yet?"

I tried to hide my embarrassment. He possessed my primal

secrets and dispersed them on paper, and as a result, I could see evidence in his eyes that we had bonded at least from his solitary perspective. I had always considered him the enemy, the force I had to work against in order to churn out my story. But he had interpreted our relationship differently. It was almost insulting, to be truthful. He wasn't my friend, and I was never interested.

Very rudely, I made my way to the cellular phone. Once again, no message or indication of a missed call. Only my picture, the time, and the little harp symbol of the mobile phone company.

"Can I come in? Once I heard the news, I was so excited I couldn't sleep. I thought you would be the same. Well, I mean, I assumed you would be happy too. We did well. We were good together," he said, romanticizing our endeavour.

Spector's voice swung in pitch from professional to personal. I couldn't pinpoint a definite intention yet, and maybe he couldn't either. I was dressed in my see-through nightgown waiting for a call, and now the news had come from the wrong messenger. I searched for a heavier robe to cover-up, but my feet had swelled, and I was experiencing heat flashes more frequently now. The baby was asleep and not moving or kicking. It simply floated in the peaceful waters of my belly.

"Please, I'm sorry."

I waved him in, anyways. He closed the door and didn't remove his hat. I wondered why he wore it. I had grown accustomed to his thinning hair. He was presenting himself as someone I didn't recognize. It was difficult to disguise a ghost, I thought, or make friends with it.

"It's authentic," he said, raising the bag. "Fish."

"I can't. The baby. I'm sorry. It's the mercury."

"I didn't realize. Perhaps Tessa might eat it."

"She's anorexic of late. Too much on her mind I guess, but maybe she will."

"How about a glass of wine?"

I didn't answer him.

"Let me guess, the baby." For a writer, he knew little about mothering. I presumed he had never married. I had never asked him about his personal life before. Ghosts weren't supposed to be married, or have children, or forge human relationships. According to the legends I read, they were supposed to float into people's lives, seek vengeance for whatever troubled them, and then rest in peace. There must be many ghosts in Iraq, I thought. Paul must be surrounded by them. At once, I hated the ghostwriter and the company he provided me. He represented another agenda, another messy loose end in the narrative of my life. The very thought of it sickened my perpetual appetite.

"Fetal alcohol syndrome," I said.

He gave me a look like I was playing too hard to get. So I walked over to him and took the flowers.

"I'll put these in water. Have a seat. I was hoping to hear from Timothy, but your news will have to do."

He took a seat on the sofa in line with my cellular phone, waiting for me to place the narrow vase holding the five carnations between them. The flowers were old and artificially red. A nice thought he now seemed to regret after seeing how they barely occupied the vase. I sat across from him and brought my legs together. I placed my hands on them.

"So?"

"It was a long and hard fight for it. But it sold to Niagara Books, well into six figures."

Although the news was exciting, its delivery was old and spiritless. It wasn't how I wanted it to arrive. There was a talent to delivering good news. It required the right approach or set-up. For a writer, his effort disappointed me. I expected praise before information, style before money. He had killed the romance of it all with the raw, uncivilized elements of what he thought would impress me. All of a sudden, he was a young boy trapped in an old skull, with nothing but a spirit to call his name, who spilled all of his milk, who had no mother's shoulder to cry on. He wanted me to take that place, but he couldn't whisper in my ear like Timothy and I knew that he would never be enough of a man for me. I could never see him as someone I would want to kiss, knowing full well that he dreamed of that moment himself, over and over again, and written it as someone else's pulp fiction memoir. The ghostwriter lacked subtlety above all things. He was cheap, a lower class of person not fit to have his name on a book cover.

"Carol? Did you hear what I said?"

About to send him out of the condominium, I jumped from a louder knock that shook the room, awakening the baby inside of me. I could feel it swimming now. Long, excited strokes to the shore of my hips.

I quickstepped my way to the door without excusing myself. Timothy heaved hungry breaths in the frame. He had returned sweaty from a corporate war. His tie was askew, his vest unbuttoned, and dark rings framed his eyes. His hair had permanently gelled into a curl, and his expensive silver suit softened to my touch when I held his arms. He squeezed my shoulders in a passionate way, like he had travelled deserts on foot to reach me.

"I ran straight here from the auction. I wanted to tell you the right way."

He invited himself in. I glanced behind him to see if he had come on a horse. He bore his own gifts. Where was his brief-case? They were inseparable. Had he forgotten it at the auction because he wanted to see me so badly?

"I brought a nightcap."

He made his way into the room lifting a bottle of red wine and a bag of food. It smelled differently to me than the ghostwriter's submission. It smelled of sharp vegetables and vitamins, not grease. Timothy still hadn't seen Conrad Spector on the sofa, until the red carnations caught his attention.

He paused before his entire energy transformed from adrenaline to attack mode. "You didn't tell her the news already, did you?"

Timothy curled into himself with disgust at the sight of Spector. He appeared ready to fight the ghost, and I felt a rush of excitement in my belly. The baby swam and laughed inside at the anticipation of conflict over its mother.

Spector stood up, appearing smaller under the shade of the cap. Younger. So obvious in his unwanted presence. He prepared himself to do something stupid, like defend me, or even something more stupid, like say something honest about Timothy, and how he was exploiting and seducing me in so many ways. Had he convinced himself with his own fiction, and if so, had he valued me in a way I could have never expected? Had he fallen in love with his recreation of me as an innocent victim? He took a step closer to Timothy with no fear of death in his eyes. I had to interrupt.

"No, he didn't tell me the news. He has a lot of work left to do, writing it out and all, and he was just taking a break."

Conrad Spector stared at me for a long time. We stood, watching him as he fit the puzzle together in his brain. He knew that I was not the character he created. He could not guess how willingly I would walk into the darkness with Timothy. Perhaps he once considered himself my only escape route, a halfway marker on the road back to humanity. But I didn't want him in my story.

He split the space between Timothy and I, and walked a line out the door. I could neither hear his steps down the stairwell nor the opening of the elevator doors. He floated away or perhaps descended to the ground. I rushed over to the door to close and lock it.

Timothy flicked through the bag of food Spector had delivered.

"What does he think you are, a dog? You are pregnant for Heaven's sake. You can't eat this." He picked it up with the tips of his fingers and dropped the bag in front of the dog, who had taught herself to sleep with her eyes open. A new trick of playing dead that she devised on her own.

"And what kind of man brings a woman vinegar," Timothy

said, laughing as he read the label on the bottle of wine. He brought it over to the sink, rummaged to find a corkscrew, and then poured the entire bottle down the drain.

"Oh, what a stink. He expected you to drink this? You can't even cook with it."

I listened to the gurgle of the wine, relieved I didn't have to drink it, worried it would stain the stainless steel of the sink. And then I remembered and turned my attention to the dark bottle of wine Timothy had left on my entrance table. Was he going to force me to drink some? Would I seem impolite if I refused any offer from the man who made me a millionaire overnight? He would never do anything to harm his prize client. He would preserve me and my baby as best he could, like any good stepfather.

As he set the table, he smiled at me in a more personal way. "Are you happy?"

"Yes."

"It's a lot of money," he said. "Now you can live your life."

What prevented me from living it now? Then I remembered Paul trapped in an Iraqi prison. Had his kidnapping freed me to live a life of my own? Why wasn't I feeling guilty about such thoughts? It felt too natural to think of myself, or my baby for that matter. Or had I accepted he would die? Was this my way of getting over him before there was anything to get over? A defense mechanism intended to keep the mourning widow away.

"I like bearing good news, Carol. There's something special about making something out of nothing, and then sharing it with someone special."

This prologue introduced a more personal narration. "You know, when I was a boy I dreamed of a time when I could walk into a room and light up a woman's beautiful face. I was full of pimples then, and I had psoriasis and all kinds of skin problems. My mother had thought someone cursed or plagued me with boils. She said that, 'Children should be seen and not heard,' but I should be neither. She didn't want me to go to school. I was an embarrassment to her. So I stayed home and read books all day. I read them and read them over and over again until I threw up words. As a result of my devotion to them, I could feel my tongue grow longer and sharper with every word I memorized."

Timothy turned around. His tongue exited his mouth in a playful manner. It was long and sharp as he described it, and he wiggled it around to amuse me. I was captivated by this story of his insecurities. The buildup led me to a calm place where he would bless me with the news from the auction. He was romanticizing the moment, and I was enjoying the suspense. So was the baby.

"You see, when I was very young I was my mother's golden baby. I was perfect, and she told everyone so. She put me into commercials, and I made her lots and lots of money. She gave pictures of me to all of her friends. My face was on boxes of baby cereal, and they dressed me up to star in films. I was a scene-stealer, and all of the other actors hated me."

With corkscrew in hand, Timothy made his way over to his bottle of wine. The screw was sharp on all edges and pointed at the end, like his tongue. As he narrated, he thrust the pointed part into the cork and his words grinded as the screw made its way to open air.

"But one day, all of these pimples covered me. I was a teenager, and everyone thought I was ugly. I was no longer the bright star of the baby commercials. We didn't get many calls, and I refused to do the work I could find, which was mostly 'before' pictures in acne cream commercials. My mother decided to take what little money remained from my younger days and invest it in my brother, who had always been jealous of my career. She had written him off because of me, but suddenly, he was the beautiful one with the potential to save the family's lifestyle."

His anger twisted the corkscrew. I thought the bottle was going to explode.

"So I ran away. I tried to get into various schools, but they wouldn't accept me without a diploma. To this day, I think it was because of the way I looked. The only people to accept me were those recruiting for the army. They welcomed me to war, and I went and killed for them in Bosnia. Then I came home, and now I kill for myself. With my tongue."

He laughed, and the cork popped. I could see a soft vapour release from it like another ghost.

Timothy retrieved some glasses and delicately placed them aside one another on the table. He struck a match to light the decorative candle. I never wanted to light that candle; it was too beautifully laced with pearls to be used. He unwrapped the food. A stronger scent invaded the air. "I brought us sushi."

He poured the wine into the glasses. He hadn't even mentioned the auction yet, and I tried hard to forget the news the ghost had delivered me in order to grace his narrative with sincerity. I instructed my mind to forget it, and then I pinched myself when I found it hard to do so. I wanted to appear surprised. Timothy had taken such efforts to romanticize it for me. He had eliminated the enemy, confessed his heart, and brought gifts to enhance the mood. I was worried about fetal alcohol syndrome. I was worried about mercury in the fish. I was worried about raw fish and botulism. But he was worried about me and what I thought of him, and that was all that mattered at the moment. Even my husband, so many levels of fear away although close to me in the pictures on the wall, and even closer to me in the protection of my womb, couldn't convince me otherwise. Timothy noticed something in my observation of him and read it appropriately.

"I know what you're thinking. Don't worry. A few glasses of wine will not harm you. I've read up on it. Pregnant women are permitted a few glasses of wine; it's good for the baby. Trust me. And this fish doesn't have mercury. If anything, it will make the baby smarter due to the high content of essential fatty acids and omega-threes. Like I said, I've ready many good books. All of those authors in your collection on the coffee table are clients of mine."

He pulled a chair back for me. The sky lightened to a cerulean grey. He raised his glass of wine, hinting with the gesture for me to do the same.

"A toast. To Carol Shell, the newest celebrity author who recently sold her book to Niagara Publishing for a record two million dollar advance."

Although I had failed to forget the ghostwriter's previous announcement, I did my best to feign surprise. I forced myself to laugh hysterically, before placing my hand over my mouth. Before long I was crying and willing myself to do so. I was creating this emotion, I was creating these tears, and I was in control of my destiny. My life was becoming a film under my own direction, and I maintained the emotional tenor of it. Timothy also smiled proudly.

Not to insult him or curse the toast, I put the glass of wine to my mouth and took a hearty sip. I couldn't help to imagine something mysterious swirling in the glass like a spirit and it was entering my body now and making its way to the clean ocean where my baby swam. The baby calmed its kicking after I placed the glass down.

His cellphone rang. It was the same ring tone that marked his calls on my phone.

"It's late at night. I told you to call me early in the morning if I didn't get back to you tonight. Yes, I've contacted him. He wants to meet you too. He's supposed to call me tomorrow. Like I said, don't worry. Listen, come by my office tomorrow, and we'll talk about it face to face. Sure, sweetie. Bye."

All of a sudden, I hated the word, *sweetie.*

"Who was that?"

I shrunk into myself to play with the raw fish on my plate, with only chopsticks at my disposal.

"You'll never believe it."

"Try me."

"This girl claims to be the daughter of the woman kidnapped with your husband."

I stopped.

"I know, amazing isn't it? I'm going to sign her on as soon as I introduce her to another client of mine."

"The woman with my husband?"

"Yes, that freelance reporter. Apparently, she's an addict, which is why your husband's employer let her go. She was also very promiscuous and dangerous, probably full of diseases. Total weirdo."

He purposefully scrunched his face as if to appear disgusted while he twiddled the chopsticks to bring a raw piece of fish to his sharp, long tongue.

"Her daughter?"

"Yeah, she's young. A runaway, I think. But beautiful. I can already see where I can take her. I'm picturing the 'poor daughter who never knew her mother' angle and then the 'poor beautiful daughter who becomes a model because she has both inner and outer beauty and her long-lost mother's strength and poise.' I can parlay that into some auditions and maybe some major film roles because she's so young and sexual. Everyone likes to see a young innocent daughter in a sexual role."

His tongue reached down to fish the next piece of sticky rice from the plate.

"I'm not hungry," I said.

"Why not? I'm starving."

He continued to eat everything in front of him, mixing it with long swigs of wine. He consumed the table with his vision, while I felt small in it all, and irrelevant, like I had assumed the role of a tree in the background. I had to do something not to lose him. I couldn't help myself.

"Do you imagine me as sexual?" I leaned over the table and thrust up the cleavage I had gained from the pregnancy. His active hunger diverted into a silent digestion. He rose from the table and extended his hand to me.

"I have always dreamed, since I was a child, of walking into a room and lighting up a woman's beautiful face."

I rose from the table, worried he would see me as pregnant, worried it would prevent him from loving me the same way, worried he would leave me for this younger girl whose mother was trapped in a room with my husband.

"I won't hurt the baby," he assured me as his tongue swirled the remnants of wine and raw fish on his lips. I tasted both when he moved in to kiss me. His tongue almost choked me. When he released himself, I nearly coughed out loud. Once he settled my breathing down with a finger to my mouth, he turned me around and wrapped his arm around my belly. I could see the light of day hiding behind buildings as he pulled up my soft nightgown and entered me. When he released his seed, I felt fear once again for my baby.

CHAPTER 17: **LEA**

I TRIED TO READ THE BOOK our captors planted in the room. But it was pitch-black, and I could find no light under the door. Again, I wondered why would they leave me a book I couldn't read? Paul heard the pages turn and rebuked me. "I told you to stay away from that book. It's written with poison ink."

"I can't even see any words, so don't worry. And what is poison ink?"

"That's the point. They're trying to lure you to their ways."

"With an illegible book?"

"With a book of spells."

I tried hard to catch even a single word in the paleness of my palms. I had seen some of the words when they opened the door the last time. A brief glance and then my body convulsed when subjected to the brightness of white light.

"I don't deserve to live," Paul moaned.

I had tolerated such complaints after every torture session and now found the unreadable book in my hands more interesting than his guilt. I had no choice but to listen.

"I didn't want to stay with her," he said. "I lived a perfect life with a perfect wife who will bear me a perfect child. She tried to get me to stay. She said I was praised and blessed in New York. Except, she never asked me the right questions. She assigned me the wrong answers instead because she knew I was harbouring the questions. She must have read my dreams. She must have read between the lines to see a man with false belief in himself. She didn't react when I told her I would report from the war zone. She was reading a book for expectant mothers at the time. She was sitting on a white sofa across from a white chair. My dog was happy. It felt like everybody could see through me but the dog."

I placed the book down on the carpet, frustrated with its Morse code-like messages, while his voice echoed from different parts of the room now.

"She fell in love with herself in me," he said, with regret.

"And you?"

The mention of his wife had spawned new interest in him. I moved closer but not close enough for him to reject me again.

"I married the time."

"The time?"

"The time of my fear. They raised me high in their eyes, at the network. And my agent, he traded in that stray bullet for my promotion. They put me in front of a camera that had my name written on it. They digitally perfected my face and retold my history so that I was a courageous journalist or a prophet shouting in an Internet wilderness. They taught me how to use a new voice, and I imitated it well. They showed me how to look into the camera, how to adjust my angles. They created me with some powder dust and a little spray and I became someone else. They buried who I was and made me into what I am and no one cried at the funeral. No one stopped them, not even my wife. She watched me die and resurrect in such a short time and I was married to it. I was married to my rebirth to the world on Channel 41. She preferred me on the screen and not in the same room."

I could see his wife with my mind's eye now. She was not pregnant, just an emptied woman, wearing a nice dress to cover the gaping hole.

"I died too. I think I even killed myself," I said in the same confessional tone of voice. I made my way a little closer, or rather, to where I heard my voice echo strongest in the room.

"Why would you do that?" he asked.

"I wasn't ready to suffer or die young. I hated the saints they made me read about in school. I hated them for being sick. All of them were young and innocent. They lived rich or poor, but then all of them became sick and died. Not one of them didn't suffer. Some had their heads cut off. Others were crucified. Others asked to be tortured more. They were crazy people, and I had heard His voice, just like they did, and I put my hands over my ears. I heard His voice loud and clear, and He was calling me to do the same, but I said no and no and no and no until I couldn't say no anymore."

"What voice are you talking about?" When he asked this question, I sensed sarcasm in his voice.

"*His* voice."

"Whose voice?"

"*His.*"

Paul laughed aloud. He was hysterical. I knew exactly where he was in the room. He couldn't stop himself. Not even when footsteps rushed to the door, and a bright light blinded us again.

"Stop it," I whispered.

"You were called by God. I have never heard anything more funny in my entire life."

One man in a full head scarf stood in the door creating a long shadow while others scurried in behind him. The effect created blended flashes on the wall. I made my way to the corner of the room where I had left the book. I grabbed it and saw words that were familiar to me. The book was written in English but the characters that spoke to God were different, more poetic. The man at the door spotted me, but he simply nodded to justify my curiosity. The sound of a drill and the scraping of a chair entered the room. Two men broke past the overseer and placed the chair in the middle of the room, underneath the hanging chains. Paul continued to laugh. I could see his rib bones rolling beneath his skin. He was a naked man laughing and laughing and laughing to infinity. Laughing at infinity.

The men loosened the leather straps bolted to the armrests of the chair. Another group of men rushed into the room. They took hold of Paul by the elbows. The older man, the sketch artist, set up shop at a fair distance from the chair. He was already sketching the prop into his book. The young boy genuflected with his video recorder. I couldn't see his beautiful eyelashes any more. It was as if he had grown out of them from the last torture session. He didn't look my way, either.

All of them ignored me as I sat in the corner with the book pressed against my chest. I wasn't sure what to pay attention to: Paul being strapped into the wooden chair or the book I was dying to read. I felt like the only one in the room without a role.

One of the taller men pulled a machine from behind his back. It wasn't attached to a cord. Grease streaks snaked around its steel bit. Paul laughed until he saw it, and then the laughter found harmony with a sudden fright and shock. When the power drill pierced the air around him, his laughter receded to the shore with a strong undertow of epiphany.

I looked down to the book when I figured it out. But I couldn't stop myself from watching. Two men held the chair down from the backrest as the other man with the power drill placed it on top of Paul's hand like a long nail. Paul's screams were loud enough for me to drop the book and cover my ears. The sketch artist didn't flinch. He seemed old enough in his ways not to be surprised by such a vision. He stretched his neck around, avoiding the obstacles of bodies to get a clean line of vision for the image, while his hand swept violently in strokes across the page in the book. The young boy holding the camera inched closer on bended knees to capture the symbolic intention of this episode. Paul passed out when they drilled through his feet.

CHAPTER 18: CAROL

WHEN I WOKE UP IN THE EARLY MORNING I was still pregnant, but something had changed. I approached the mirror framed above the espresso-coloured dresser. Timothy lay asleep on top of the decorative duvet, on my husband's side. His long tongue had slipped out to coat the pillow with a wet spot of drool. Seeing my image in the mirror, I concluded I had been sleeping the whole time, trapped in the residual effects of a dream that slowly gave way to a nightmare. Now, the morning frost of reality approached. The sounds of traffic outside pinched me with the truth, and I knew I had aged overnight.

Perhaps they were always there and I hadn't noticed, but wrinkles now creased my eyes and new laugh lines framed my mouth. I stretched them out with a hand. In the mirror, a goblin's face laughed back at me. Timothy moaned in his sleep. He often spoke during the night. Selling names. Selling ideas. Selling himself. I locked the door to keep the dog out. Last night, when we first entered the bedroom to sleep, Tessa finally woke up from her malaise. She growled outside the door while Timothy spoke in his sleep. I could not press my eyelids down. I tried to listen to the baby swimming inside of me, above the growling, but the baby back-floated in silence. Asleep or angry for unwelcome company in her conception bed. I tried to whisper apologies to her or him, but Timothy's sleep-talking always interrupted me. He rolled over and his hand accidentally slipped in-between his legs. He rubbed himself at times, in his deeper sleep, unconscious of the crudeness of this act. So I woke up, only to find I couldn't recognize the woman in the mirror anymore. In the reflection of the mirror, his eyes remained closed, although he could still read my thoughts.

"I have an incredible dermatologist. A true artist." Timothy's voice escaped, muffled, as he spoke into my goose-feathered pillows.

His tongue slurped its way into his mouth again as he turned and sat up in the reflection of the mirror, scratching himself under the covers. "His name is Dr. Dean. We call him Dr. D., or D-day."

"What happened to me, Timothy?"

I inspected my hands. They had dried out. Timothy played with his cellphone now. It rang all of a sudden, like he had programmed it to do so, purposely.

"No, I haven't forgotten about you."

He laughed and stretched his spine by kicking the duvet from the bed. I had not seen the tattoo on his shoulder the night before. A green demon in a military uniform. He arose, scratching himself violently. Must have been the coarseness of shaven or lasered skin. His motions were inverted in the mirror. He had no hair on his body other than that on his head. He was a newborn adult. Clean and unscathed but for the tattoo. Not a single imperfection or mole to raise alarms of insecurity. He made his way to the window to stretch, spreading his arms and legs to their full span before curling one arm back to his head to speak into the phone.

"Like I said, I cleared my morning for you, remember. I scratched out everything for your story. I'll see you there, and we can talk about it then.... I assure you, there is a lot of untapped potential in this situation. All you have to do is say yes.... Xavier won't be in town until the Prayer and Protest Festival. You can meet him there." Timothy paused, then the conversation continued. "Yes.... Of course.... Is the hotel taking care of you? How is the room?... Well, remember, you're in New York now, so be careful.... Yes.... Leave the rest to me.... See you soon."

His phone snapped closed.

"I've got to get back to the office, Carol."

"Was that your younger client?" I asked his reflection in the mirror. It was difficult to control the dusting off of new discoveries on my face. He had grown younger overnight, while I saw distinct traces of hair on my face, liver spots on my hands, and temple wrinkles.

"Yes, she needs to meet with me right away. I think she's scared. That's twice she's called me. She's practically obsessed with one of my clients, Xavier Means."

He dressed himself from the top down as he offered an overly detailed explanation for his hurried exit. The process, which involved seeing his lower body exposed and upper body covered by a shirt, annoyed me.

"I can't believe my eyes," I said to myself. He overheard me.

"Like I said, I will refer you to Dr. D. He's the best dermatologist in New York."

"But I'm pregnant, Timothy." I emphasized the bulging reality by squaring out the area with my hands.

"He has a lot of clients who are pregnant. The Botox goes into your eye socket and cheeks, not your blood, and he's a master with a laser."

"Laser?"

"Yup. Look what he's done to me. I'm baby clean, no hair." He spun around to show me.

I pressed my hands to my face again. My skin had lost some tension. I wanted to blame him because he was in the room. I wanted to blame his semen inside of me, which could have been diseased for all I knew with an STD or the plague. My baby might have been infected by it. Or maybe the baby was hiding on a distant shore somewhere, cast away. He approached to bring me close to him in the elastic trap of his arms.

"Trust me, Carol. You are a celebrity now. Every one of them gets a little work done from time to time. And God knows you have the money to splurge now. If you like, I'll call Dr. D. and let him know you're coming."

"What about the Ironstone girl?"

"What about her?"

"Are you going to leave me for her?"

His face shrunk in confusion.

"Like I said, I'll give him a call and make an appointment. We've got to get you ready for the Prayer and Protest Festival. I'm sure every media outlet is going to want to interview you, most especially the Daytime Diva."

I smiled and conceded, while he dressed quickly and left the condominium without breakfast or petting the dog. I wanted to call him on his cellphone, but I needed to pee him out first.

CHAPTER 19: **LEA**

"THEY ARE BURNING. The holes are burning." Paul shivered as I tightened the cloths wrapped on his hands and feet. The blood had soaked through. I was worried that the depths of the holes in his hands and feet could not be contained by a scab or with a cloth.

The drill man left the room shortly after piercing through the soles of Paul's feet, only to return with a bag of torn cloths and a conciliatory plate of mush. Before then, they had loosened Paul from the straps of the chair and let him drop to the sewer hole below it. They removed the chair from the room. And then the door closed.

I palmed my way through streaks of blood and the scent of herbs to reach him. The ground was warm and silky wet on my hands. He was whimpering and crying to himself. The sound was raspy and tragic and historical, like a child who had scraped his knee for the first time, awakening his vulnerability. My first touch on his back made him flinch. The pain almost glowed from his hands.

"Stay away from me, please. I am begging you."

I felt around the floor for the bag of cloths. When I found it, I crawled back to him.

"I'll wrap them tight to stop the bleeding."

"Please, let me bleed away into the sewer."

"I can't let you do that."

"Why not? They didn't do it to *you*."

I turned away from him. They had spared me this time, and for some reason I felt more horrible for it, like Paul had stolen my purpose. For years, I had visualized these scenes. Observed myself and myself only as the subject of what I believed to be predestined sufferings. To endure it with someone else was an education. I understood its significance by watching Paul suffer more than I did this time. I felt pity and a surge of emotion only releasable by tears. It reminded me I was human. Not just a spirit trapped within a cold skeleton. I was human with a place inside that hurt when it watched greater suffering than it experienced. I was still jealous of him, but the envy carried a weight to it. It was attached to a heavy place inside of me, rooted deeply in associations, memories and childhood experiences, like the last time I felt this way. When my father died. And before they buried him.

Paul curled up on the ground. I extended my body warmth to him.

"I told you to stay away," he said.

"I can't do that, Paul. Not now."

I dropped my face to his chest and kissed it. I kissed him everywhere softly. His refusals lightened.

"Please."

"Don't worry," I said. "There is more to our poetry than remembered words."

I made my way with soft kisses to the bulging cloths on his feet. They were blood-soaked as well, and I could taste his blood, which resembled the aftertaste of wine in my mouth.

Skin bumps spread across his body like a pestilence. I kissed my way up his legs.

"Only say the word and I will be healed," he repeated as if hypnotized himself by a former association.

I kissed him better, as a mother would, and he whimpered until he forgot the burning holes in his hands and feet, until his tongue surrendered language for the immediate relief of physical connection.

He released his breath into my mouth, and I swallowed him whole. In my imagination, I believed I would give birth to his likeness in another lifetime, in a foreign desert with foreign men covered in scarves and women disappearing beneath black sheets. I swallowed the life of his air and my voice was wet with him. I kissed my way to his chest again. His bloodied hands cooled the heat in my ears. He pulled me up to his lips and tasted the poison of his pain there. I had taken it from his mouth as I would venom from a snake bite.

Our therapy was soon interrupted by men standing over us. They had come to take their turn with me. Others proceeded to hang him on the criss-crossed chains above the sewer.

CHAPTER 20: CAROL

I SAT IN FRONT OF MY COMPUTER SCREEN and clicked the mouse. After surfing for "globe news related topics' on my browser for the tenth time in as many minutes, I accepted my predestined fate. I had not lost my spot to my husband, despite what I had seen of the new torture tapes released on his news channel. The people preferred my story to his and the other woman's. The video tried to upstage me, but I survived its novel attack.

Timothy hadn't called yet. He promised he would do so after he left the number of his dermatologist behind. It felt cheap, but I liked his bluntness where it concerned my physical improvement. The condition of my face prompted a verifiable emergency. I had aged overnight, and an internal force had taken the reigns of my youth, kidnapping my pregnant glow and replacing it with a new, dull mask.

Deep down, I blamed Timothy for the whole thing. He blamed himself as well, which is why he was so generous with his referral. I sat on the toilet for nearly an hour hoping that his semen would fall out of me before accepting more of it into my system. In my imagination, it settled inside of me, influencing the weather of my hormones, storming the front of my guilt.

Tessa couldn't open her eyes this morning. I worried she had died until she moaned when I turned on the news. Her suffering continued, and her body deteriorated on the floor before a bowl full of decomposing scraps. Her appetite had gone for good.

I considered calling Timothy and asking him if he knew of a dog psychologist, but I decided against it. He would definitely think I was finding an excuse to hear his voice. He wouldn't appreciate my desperation, most especially if it interrupted his meeting with the Ironstone girl. He trotted away with a hop in his step when he left the condominium, like he could do no wrong, like he controlled the elements.

I typed my name in another search engine. I did this countless times in the course of a day. For all of Timothy's hoopla, I had little to do when he wasn't around.

A list appeared with my name in bold blue type. I clicked the next button and another list appeared. I clicked it again and was flattered by another one. By the fifth page, my husband's name appeared alongside mine. It took him five pages to reach me. So, things hadn't changed all that much. This one particular link contained the banns of marriage for every intended couple at Saint Alexandria Church, including our own. Our affluent church must have found a means to enter irrelevant information into the new millennium.

I closed the search and returned to the mirror. My new reflection made me panic at the precarious thought of my husband's return. My face appeared glossy and in need of powder, and worst of all, I couldn't control the way my pores emptied perspiration.

If Paul were to see me like this, would he recognize me? Would I appear like the mother of his child or as some fabricated version better equipped for the front cover of *Cosmopolitan.* Worse yet, would he see through me?

As I leaned in closer to the mirror, I could see new stories on the surface, which he would be able to read instantly. The words had found new lines in the wrinkles to string themselves together and form a story of regret. I found the slip of paper Timothy had left me and called Dr. D. To his secretary, I claimed it was an emergency and requested an appointment right away.

CHAPTER 21: LEA

AS THEY STRUNG PAUL UP LIKE A PUPPET from the ceiling, I realized our torturers were creating stories with our bodies. The room became a printing house in Hell, and we were the blank pages in which knowledge or content would be transmitted from generation to generation.

A man with a different head scarf organized this torture session. The scarf covered his entire face except for his eyes. I had never seen light in a man's eyes like these in Baghdad. They were ice-blue. He had immigrated. He was once a soldier from my homeland, I was sure of it. A traitor. His eyebrows were light as well. Dirty blond.

Paul didn't notice. His head dropped to his chest, nearly covering the cross there. He begged them to stop, speaking under his breath with all of the energy he could muster. Blood dripped to his fingertips and congealed in the nails. On his elevated feet, I could see lines of blood tattooing the spaces between his toes.

When the light-eyed man turned around, I noticed the scarf was strung in a heavy knot in the back, making it appear as if the man had grown a mane. Video cameras floated in a circle about the area, coordinated by the young technician. His scarf was gone now, and I could see his delicate features ruffled in concentration as he directed the callused hands of the older, clumsier men. Stronger men from behind me pulled me higher so that my feet wouldn't touch the floor. The more I dangled them, the more the chains gripped my shoulders. The sketch artist pencilled the scene once again from a corner. I was growing curious, wanting to see his images and to know why he had secluded us all in the same book.

Paul's collarbone must have been broken. His head was too heavy for him to lift and face me.

In another corner of the room, the woman in the brown frock sat on the carpet reading the book they had left for me, waiting, it seemed, for the show to officially start. She only existed in the light. But not to anyone else in the room. They walked by her without acknowledging her begging presence. I spoke to her. "What are you doing here?"

The man with the scarf mane sneered hot breath like a Dragon. He cleared the ground and pulled a water hose into the room. The videographers moved in for a close-up of the prop. The woman in the monk's frock raised her head from the book to watch. She didn't answer me.

The Dragon Man gave a hand signal to a man outside the door.

I could hear the water rumbling through the rubber hose. The Dragon Man pointed the cavernous tube at me and it spouted forth, denting my skin. The push of the water made the chains above tingle like wind chimes. He sprayed my entire body. Some of the water's sediment had found its way into my mouth. It tasted like rubber and rust. They showered Paul the same way, but he didn't raise his head. Another man pulled a chain, vaulting him higher into the air. Paul's chin remained buried in his chest, just above the spot where they had branded the cross onto his skin with a flat iron.

More lights flooded the room with other spectators holding them high. After having soaked us completely, the light-eyed man slid his hand across his neck. The message was passed in a similar gesture to a line of scarves along the wall to the door. The water abruptly retreated leaving only a trickle in its absence. Like a paramedic, the leader of this session received two metal pads attached to red wires. He made another signal with them. A humming noise from a power generator rumbled behind me. I scanned the area below me only to see the hose in a perfect slithering position, like a viper about to rise and sting my feet. Other, lighter eyes sidestepped their way into the room to observe. They stood apart from the regular scarves on the other side of the room. They were there to watch their own leader, observe him, and enjoy his magic show.

The woman in the brown frock rose to her feet for the anthem. The Dragon Man pulled the part of the scarf covering his chin so that he could breathe into the open air. I saw a sharp, shaved chin. He snapped the metal pads together, and the lights in the room dimmed.

I focused on the woman in the brown robe. "What is happening to me?" I asked.

The woman in the brown robe refused to speak. I saw others enter the room, although not from the door. They stood on either side of Paul. They were winged men, angelic. I assumed the Dragon Man hadn't seen them yet. He walked by them without acknowledging their intrusion on his space. Another man with a scarf whipped Paul's back with a steel wire so that he would lift his head and watch. He needed to face the camera.

The Dragon Man pressed the metal pads onto my wet skin.

The lights dimmed.

My head shook.

My bones rattled in unison with the chains.

My teeth shivered.

Paul screamed.

The leader removed the pads from my body, and applause broke out in the room to fill the silent spaces. The two angels didn't clap. Neither did the woman in the robe. She walked closer to me, removing her hood. Her face shone a laundered white. I had seen it before, in a book. The cheeks blossomed, blush pink, as if on cue. Her hair softened to a lighter brown. The angels remained still, watching her approach. Respectful.

"Why won't you talk to me?" I asked her.

The applause died down. The video cameras moved in while the Dragon Man raised his electric talons above his head. He pressed them into me. The chains above me shook and rattled to a diminishing sound, like trickling water. Paul hung still, dripping blood into the sewer one drop at a time. When the Dragon Man pulled the pads away, the woman in the brown robe approached me in his spot.

"You are called again," she finally said, in the way I imagined my daughter would speak.

"Called?"

The woman nodded. She walked away. The Dragon Man returned. His mouth frothed at the edges. His lips charred red with fire. When he placed the metal pads on my wet body, I shook and screamed and bit my tongue. The smell of burnt hair on my body clouded the air. The nerves beneath my skin sizzled and seized.

The woman in the brown robe approached me again. "You have failed to answer it."

She walked out of the room. The angels followed her. Paul hadn't moved or motioned to notice her. He couldn't see the angels either.

"Kill me. I beg you. Kill me," he said, provoking the lot of them.

This new terrorist ignored him. He returned and placed the pads on my body again.

My head snapped back. I could feel the electricity rushing through my body, shaking the dusted contents stored within. Fragile memories I had collected and protected, hidden and packaged in tissue and stored in the closet of my regrets, shattered to the ground of my remembrance. I was a young girl and a little boy had chased me home from school on his bike. I tried to run away from him, but he caught up to me and spat in my face. I cried, but he continued to spit in my face. I couldn't even see where I was running. I didn't know where home was. I called for my father, but I knew he was below ground. The boy reminded me of it as he spat on my face. I fainted into the arms of a woman at the side of the road. The boy had disappeared. The clicking of the bicycle chain no longer chased me. Its sound disappeared in the distance.

In my bed, my mother had told me about the woman who brought me home. She described her face as porcelain, like one of the angels in her religious collection of statuettes in the dining room hutch.

CHAPTER 22: CAROL

T HE DERMATOLOGIST WORE A BOW TIE with a tweed
jacket. He walked into the white waiting room to greet me
with an apology. "I'm sorry to hear about your husband, but
I'm certainly honoured to meet such a courageous woman."

I smiled as I gave him my hand with the wedding ring. He
took it in his and helped me up from the chair. I followed his
clean scent to one of the inspection rooms. He was a tall man
with a long stride. When he closed the door, his voice dropped
to a whisper. "So, I understand you're one of Timothy's girls."

I nodded as he pressed his thumbs into my cheeks. His breath
was sharp and fruity. His skin resembled a sheet of faintly
spotted velvet. He squeezed a magnifying glass into his eye
socket and rolled himself closer until we nearly kissed at the
nose. "Okay, I see why you're here."

I held my breath.

He rolled back to his desk to write down some notes. "Your
face tells quite a story."

He pulled a stronger magnifying glass from a shelf above.
"Your pigments are like pages of history," he said, losing
himself in his own whimsy.

"You sound like Timothy."

"We get along well. We understand the ways of the world."

"Really?"

"Yes. We both see you as a story. I hide the ones you don't
want to tell, and Timothy sells the ones you do. For example,

I can see faint acne scars that could use a chemical peel on your next visit."

"And what do you make of them?"

"Internal conflict. An insecurity with natural light."

I flinched as the bright beam blared through the magnifying glass. He was right. I had always applied concealer if I knew I would be seen in daylight. When I was younger, I would go to different rooms in my home to see if the scars were less visible. One time, I punched a mirror and shattered it into a million little pieces when I realized this one acne scar would never go away.

"Over here, there are freckles you've been covering with makeup for years. A conflicted inheritance. You don't talk to your parents much anymore, do you?"

I wouldn't give him the pleasure of confirming his analysis.

"These ... now these are reactive wrinkles ... not real ones," he explained.

His soft thumb pressed into my temples.

"Reactive wrinkles?"

"Yes. Sometimes, our faces react to what's happening within us. Our skin is layered like palimpsest. The messages appear from the inside out."

"So, you're telling me that my body is reacting to something and showing the reaction on my face?"

"Precisely. But these are deep. Deep, deep reactive wrinkles." He was lost again in his own theory. "I can see why Timothy referred you to me."

He pulled the magnifying glass back, the glass eye popped out into his hand.

I wasn't happy.

"What do the wrinkles represent?" I said, assuming him to be more apt as a psychic reader than skin specialist. I was growing impertinent, I realized, but I didn't care. The dermatologist laughed.

"Not to worry, Mrs. Shell."

He showed me a needle.

"My patients come and see me because they are interested in erasing those stories. My patients are modernists. They don't want the sunken cathedrals and palaces of the past, they want the hot new skyscrapers. So I build them what they want. Or, at least, I renovate."

"Is that what you would call yourself, doctor? A renovator?"

Dr. D. wiped his hands on his face in slow, silky strokes.

"I lasered my entire face. Not one speck of hair will grow back where I don't want it to grow back."

"Why would you do such a thing?"

"I live a life of convenience, like everyone else, only I devote myself to it."

"Convenience?"

"Yes. The physical removal of the past is the key to living a life of convenience. It's hard to feel unhappy if you don't see history in the mirror. If we cast aside all of the inhibitions that link us to time and we replace them with the most efficient paths to pleasure, we kill time and become masters of it."

Dr. D. rose from his seat to grab a plastic bottle missing its label. It rested with a group of others below a storage cupboard.

He chuckled as he shook the bottle. "From acne to eternity in five easy sentences. I like that speech, don't you?"

"What do you recommend I do, Doctor?"

"I am going to inject this underneath the wrinkles so that they'll flatten and become smooth."

"What is it?"

"A solution to perception. Fluid beneath the skin."

"You know I am pregnant, doctor?"

"There are no side effects to beauty, Mrs. Shell."

I smiled.

"When I am finished with you, you will feel like you are wearing a mask for a few days. People will call you porcelain and admire you as they would a statue rising from a fountain."

The needle approached my eye.

"Does Timothy send all of his girls to you?" I asked.

"Only the beautiful ones."

"Why?"

"Because ugly is just a bad story to begin with."

The needle pierced my skin and I could feel the liquid settling behind my eye. His thumb pressed into the swelling to spread it. After he finished both sides, he opened the window to let in the daylight. He placed a mirror before me. The reactive wrinkles I had awoken to and the old acne scar had flattened to the bone. My face froze into a figurine. Smooth, soft, and accentuated, with new bone structure.

"What are you doing with that?" I asked again.

He shook a can and tested the spray into a rag.

"Take your clothes off," he demanded.

"Excuse me?"

"I am going to spray you with this, and we will go to the tanning room."

"The tanning room?"

"Yes, the machine is built into the walls. All you have to do is stand for five minutes."

"Is it safe?"

"It's only light, Mrs. Shell."

I hesitantly removed my dress.

"All of your under clothes. Now raise your arms out to your sides."

When I lifted them, he began to spray. The artificial scent of the mist nearly choked me.

"Now follow me."

I followed Dr. D. into a cylindrical chamber of long, fluorescent bulbs.

"I'll be back soon."

Dr. D. exited, closing the door behind him, encasing me in darkness. A switch snapped, and the miracle of light surrounded me.

CHAPTER 23: **CAROL**

TIMOTHY ARRANGED A LIMOUSINE to drive me to the Prayer and Protest Festival. He convinced me I needed to carry myself like a celebrity in order to be one. There wasn't much else to it. The limousine driver stared at me in the rearview mirror. His fixated attention bothered me, making me feel like a snob. "Can I help you?" I snapped.

"Are you all right, lady?"

"Of course I am."

"You look cold. Do you want more heat?"

"I have enough heat, thank you."

I pressed the button above my head, prompting a black screen to separate us. In the reflection of the tiny television set embedded in the wall, I regarded my newly designed features. My cheekbones remained elevated and I glowed again, although every time I swallowed, I felt nauseous. The limousine driver braked and accelerated in jumps as we neared the protest. The ground vibrated, people walked alongside the limousine, accidentally bumping into it, rocking it, screaming out loud, alarming the baby. I pulled out a sheet of paper from my purse. Many times the night before, in front of the mirror, I had rehearsed my lines to see how the words presented themselves from the origin of my new face. The injections did indeed make it feel like a mask, a porcelain mask with jutting cheekbones and bright, glossy makeup. Ready for the masquerade.

I turned on the television set and although the signal produced a rough and fuzzy screen, my husband's new image dominated the news. He hung from chains in the newest video. They scourged, electrocuted, and tortured him beyond my spite for our failed relationship. And just I as I was about to feel pity, they showed the other woman, who shared his tortures.

In some self-delusional way, they had cheated on me. They had shared intimate moments in another land, while I gracefully dealt with the staged circus act my life had become. Just keep riding the elephant in your glittering outfit and with your arms extended out, Carol. *Ta da*! Cue the applause and pat the elephant with affection to show the crowd you are not afraid of the enormous beast.

"The terrorists are threatening to kill one of them if their demands are not met," announced the news host in a deep, bass tone.

My lungs rose in my chest as I held my breath and observed my resurrected reflection transposed onto his ugly transformation. My lungs heaved tears up, and I finally wanted to cry. I could feel the swell of them in my eyes but not the control in my facial nerves to release them.

Up until this moment, I had not been able to feel him in the room. He was always over there, becoming more and more fictional with every passing day and with every new angle to his story. And here I was, in a sailing limousine with the crushing sensation that I couldn't escape him.

I reached for a tissue from the box by the champagne glasses, but I didn't need it. The water dried up, froze in the space between my eyelid and eyeball. I pulled a portable mirror from my purse. My makeup withstood this unexpected surge of emotion, and my face remained an ice sculpture. Even the acceleration of my blinking subsided the threat of tears within seconds.

The discordant sounds of live music rose in intensity as we approached the stage, centring the concentrated crowd.

Timothy asked me not to leave the limousine until he opened the door for me. But I couldn't wait. I was suffocating within it.

CHAPTER 24: **CAROL**

I HAD FOUND THE PRAYER on the internet. The stage felt too weak to balance my heels. The lights blazed a heat trail that threatened the frozen landscape of my Botoxed face.

I read it anyway. My voice echoed in my ear.

"Lord, rescue your angels from the depths of Hell. Bring them home to the light of their homes and let them bless you with creations born in your image." I wrapped my arms around my belly. It had become my signature move. "We ask this in your name, Amen."

Cameras flashed. A television journalist waited at the bottom of the steps for my private interview. Another man stood behind him with a large camera on his shoulder. Timothy circled the area on his phone, one eye on me at all times. The circles tightened in circumference. As I moved to the camera, I felt a violent spasm in my belly. Miraculous timing, almost too good to be real. I was happy when my water broke on television, in this spectacle of light and noise and interest.

I had stolen the festival for my own. Even Timothy couldn't create such perfect timing. I was willing it to happen. I was hoping it would happen. I was making it happen.

And best of all, everyone would watch.

CHAPTER 25: **LEA**

I TRIED TO INSPIRE PAUL'S ATTENTION, but he was trapped within himself. They had shocked him again. He didn't scream out loud anymore. His screams echoed from within him, forming bubbles beneath his skin. Sometimes, they boiled like algae blooms to the surface. Mostly, they didn't.

"Paul, are you awake?"

He hung from the chains across from me, his head pinned to his chest like a poppy. He hadn't moved for hours. I swivelled my hips to gain the momentum to swing from my chains. I kicked the air until I scratched his leg with my toenail. He didn't flinch. I kicked him in the stomach, but he didn't groan. His sleep was deep. His eyes closed. At once, I panicked.

"Help! Please help me. He's dying! He's dying!"

The door opened slowly and quietly. The young boy, the camera technician, entered the room alone. He surreptitiously slid inside through the crack in the door and left it open to avoid the clank of its closing, reducing the seeping light to a thin yellow line that shot to the opposite wall. I could see murky swirls of chaos floating in the shaft of light, scattered by the tiniest movements of my captor. His tanned skin was a dull stain on the cream scarf, most of which hung behind him from a knot.

"He's dying," I whispered to him.

He believed me. He reached up and placed a hand on Paul's neck. I watched him searching for the pulse with his shiny skeletal fingers. He stuck them finally to an area to the right of Paul's chin. He turned around to face me. I softened my voice again.

"Is he alive?"

He nodded. When his eyes stared up at me, I could see their whiteness and not his beautiful eyelashes. Had he lost them in battle?

"What are you preparing us for?" I kept my whisper.

He glanced at the crack in the door as if fearing an ear on the other side. He spoke under his breath.

"Are you hungry? I can get you some food and water."

"I asked you a question."

He continued to look up to me. My elevated position made him appear shorter, or younger, as if I were reprimanding a toddler with my forefinger.

"You're not one of them, are you?"

He dug his hands into the pockets of his jeans.

"I can't help you," he finally said.

"We don't want your help."

The whiteness in his eyes reappeared.

"What are you preparing us for?" I asked again.

"History," he said.

"For history?"

"Your defeat is the birth of our history."

The door broke open, and another thick-bodied man stomped into the room. When he approached the young boy, he spoke over him in the same way, but in a gravelly tone.

The boy nodded, obediently, before he followed the direction of the man's arm, pointed at the door.

The creased, sweaty eyes above the scarf on this man's face told an angry, frustrated tale. He pulled a needle from his pocket. Removing the cap, he jabbed it into my arm. The drugs settled me with a sigh, igniting contracting breaths. He didn't stick around to see if I would run out of them. Instead, he left the room. In his place appeared the woman in the brown robe.

She nodded her head disapprovingly.

"'*Pitiable, foolish young woman! Consider the hot, burning dungeon thou art preparing for thyself to all Eternity, to which thou art going in such career.*'"

Her voice hailed from the poem Paul and I quoted to keep us alive, "The Marriage of Heaven and Hell."

"Do you know my eternal lot?" I asked her.

The woman nodded. She reached up and loosened the chains suspending me in the air. When I touched the cold cement with the soles of my damaged feet, my knees buckled. I fell to the floor. The woman offered me a hand covered in a brown glove with the fingers cut off. I grabbed it. It felt like Paul's hand in the bandage, soft in the middle.

"Follow me to a place you have created."

I rose to my feet and followed the woman to the door, co-incidentally unlocked. When she opened it, I feared a trap on the other side waiting for me. I followed the woman in the frock to the other side, but when I reached the second door, we entered another dimension. The woman in the brown robe led me through a church from my childhood with its waxy smell and statues of saints in the windows. As a child, I had never ventured down into the basement of my church, below the rectory. I followed the woman's bare feet down the stairs, smelling grain in the air and feeling the dust of it on my skin. Another stairway awaited us to the left. The woman in the brown robe waved me on, so I followed through cobwebs and narrow walls until the walls themselves transformed into dripping stone—the opening to a cave. The woman in the brown robe continued through a cavern until the spider webs above clung stronger on my head. I looked up to see the roots of trees. No sky. Only hairy roots.

"Do you recognize this place?" The woman in the monk's robe asked me.

"I have seen it before in a picture. It is engraved in my memory somewhere."

"It is what you believe your eternal lot to be—the manifestation of all of your fears, judgments, regrets, and guilt. But it isn't; you are loved. "

I took a seat in the twisted root of an oak. The woman climbed it and she appeared like she was flying underground, suspended in a fungus.

By degrees, we watched a gaping hole deepen beside us. Smoke rose from it. I peered down to see a black sun shining. In its heated revolution, spiders emerged from the smoke crawling after their prey, which were actually angels flying away into the infinite deep. The clouds of smoke transformed into goats with wings.

"Is this my eternal lot?" I asked her again.

"The one you preconceived. Right there, between the black-and-white spiders."

A cloud of fire burst and rolled through the deep, blackening all of the images and raging with a terrible noise. I grasped my ears. Everything had disappeared into a black tempest. The air became black and then red with blood and fire, while the roots above curled upwards in the opposite direction.

The head of Leviathan rose from the darkness. His forehead was divided into streaks of green and purple, from front to back, like those on a tiger's forehead. His mouth was open, and red gills hung just above the raging foam, tinging the black deep with beams of blood. He advanced in my direction with all the fury of his existence.

I tried to climb up a dangling root, but I kept slipping on its dampness. When I fell, I plummeted into a white room.

"Where am I now?" I asked the woman in the brown robe.

"You are no longer in the Hell you have created for yourself."

"I created that place?"

"Yes."

"And the monster?"

"Yes."

"And the spiders and the fire and the roots?"

"Yes. Inspired from a reading and your faith in that reading."

"Where am I now?"

"In Hell."

"This is Hell?"

"This is nothing," explained the woman in the monk's robe. "Hell is nothing. It's the aftermath of destruction, the translation of something into nothing. The ashes of a story."

"I don't understand."

The woman walked around the white room. It depicted the torture room, bleached white, but Paul wasn't there. He was hiding against the white wall, camouflaged by its plainness.

"When you cease to create, you destroy. There must be a creator and a destroyer. Those who create invent life. Those who destroy annihilate life," she explained.

"I am a destroyer," I said.

"You are a creator," the woman said with assurance.

"How do you know?"

"Hell is nothing. God is I am."

"I am not God."

"You exist buried within yourself. Your body is not a tomb, but a temple of stories."

"I can't feel a thing," I said.

"If there is too much something, there is a thirst for nothing. If there is too much nothing, there is a thirst for something. You are always thirsty. The balance is divine."

"The balance of contraries?" I asked.

"Precisely. Where there has been no story, you have told one. Where there has been nothing, you have created life. Death is the destruction of story. Life is the creation of one. Conscience is the remembering. Guilt is the regret of destruction. Redemption is the rewriting. Suffering inspires it. Suffering is the quill."

"Heaven is creation," I whispered.

"And Hell is not," the woman whispered in return.

"The story is the balance," I said.

"The story is the marriage," the woman said.

"The story is creating memory," I said.

"The story is remembering," the woman said, prodding me on.

"The story is the soul."

"Without story there is nothing," the woman said again, as if to reinforce my previous lesson.

I rose from the depths of the white dream. An old window with a broken pane opened the room to the outside. When they locked me in the torture room, I had dreamed of a window, more than anything else. I walked to it. The woman in the robe narrated.

"Let me show you your stories."

The woman in the brown robe lifted the window in the white room. I followed her through it and came to a narrow stairway leading to a second floor. I walked it alone. To the left of me, at the top of the stairs, I saw my grandmother's old sewing machine. It was built into a wooden table with a steel pedal that pumped power into the needle. I remembered watching my grandmother in this scene. I could hear the rhythm of the pedal. The needle crushing a thread through a piece of cloth. I made my way to the linen closet where I kept the white sheets. A military rifle leaned against the wall. It was thin, rusted. My grandfather's. I took it in my arms one day to feel the wooden grip. I could smell my grandfather behind me. I turned around, but he wasn't there. They sold the home after he died, but my mother donated the war rifle to a history teacher at a local school. I hated her for it.

When I descended the stairs, a man swooped me off the ground. I was running, out of breath, away from trouble in this memory. My grandmother was chasing me around the house with a wooden spatula. I had done something wrong, but I couldn't recall what. As I turned the corner, I was flying in the strength of his arms, and protected on his shoulders, where he placed me.

"Don't touch her," he said, in a language that I didn't recognize and yet understood. My grandmother retreated to the kitchen. The smell of garden tomatoes filtered through the air.

Outside, my grandfather raised me high enough to touch apricots in the trees. A train rattled the clouds, spreading them flat across the sky. Cars drove by, but the apricots didn't fall to the ground. I reached for one that was ripe and furry. I picked it. My grandfather kissed me. When he lowered me to the ground, I broke it in half and removed the pit. I offered him a piece, and he pushed me to eat it instead. It tasted sweet. Fresh from my hands. He walked over to the picnic table next to the garage. He pulled out a bag of tobacco and a steel box. He arranged some of the square white sheets on the table and then pinched brown tobacco leaves in piles. He rolled one and squeezed it into a hole. I wound the lever and a cigarette popped through. I smiled at him. He placed the cigarette in a pile of others in another steel box and watched me wind every one of them. From nothing into something. I wanted to do that forever. Make him watch me.

A man with a record player stationed himself on the sidewalk and played songs for my mother. He stood outside her window singing like a cat in heat. My grandfather grabbed his rifle and threatened to shoot if he didn't leave her alone. The man ran away, dropping the vinyl record. It shattered into shards once it reached the pavement. I picked up the pieces and delivered them to my grandfather, but he threw them away. To make him happy, I climbed a ladder to pick an apricot for him. I fell, and when I opened my eyes, I saw angels perched in the apricot tree. I ran in to tell him, but he was lying on the ground already. Other angels floated about his room. They called out to me. They called me to follow him through the door, but I ran to another room to hide.

In the church, I prayed before a statue of a bearded man with a heart of thorns sticking out of his chest. I prayed to Him to send my grandfather back. I promised I would do whatever he asked. I swore to never leave him if He answered me. When they lowered my grandfather into the ground, I saw him climb

CHAPTER 26: CAROL

I LEANED BACK ON THE AMBULANCE COT, beneath the seat belts. Timothy held my hand on one side while a stranger with a video camera sat on the other side, next to the paramedics. They had refused to let him in, but Timothy paid them.

The ambulance moved slowly at first. I could hear hands tapping it outside. A hymn started when it stopped in the midst of the crowd of people. They were singing—it was a vigil for me and the baby.

Timothy dabbed the sweat beading my forehead that I couldn't feel because of the liquid beneath my skin. The stranger rotated the focus of the lens with his other hand. I felt the picture coming closer. I felt relieved to have seen Dr. D. the day before.

"We are live," the stranger with the video camera announced.

"You're going to be all right," Timothy said, placing his second hand atop mine. He projected his voice so that it rang clear. "Don't worry. We're going to get you to the hospital as soon as we can."

Timothy's voice boomed into the ambulance from the outside speakers a moment later, repeating the sentence. A collective sigh sounded from the crowd outside the ambulance. I could hear it rumbling like an earthquake beneath the vehicle, raising it like a chariot about to take flight to another land.

Timothy cued me with his eyes to answer him. The moment inspired me to tell my own ghost story.

"I hoped he would be here for this. In the delivery room. By my side. I still remember the time I told him I was pregnant. It was in church. We were praying next to one another with our heads in our hands. I whispered in his ear that I was pregnant. The organ sounded in the loft, and the priest made his blessing. At that moment, the clouds passed, and sunlight burst through the rose window above us, and there was light all around. It was like God himself had blessed us."

I stretched my neck so I could speak directly into the lens. As I spoke, I paused for dramatic effect and to overemphasize the pain of the contractions. As a child, I was never one to show pain. When a doctor stitched up my knee without being able to freeze it beforehand, he marvelled at my threshold for pain. I didn't cry once, although I did bite my tongue with a closed mouth.

In the ambulance and in that moment of adrenaline, I couldn't feel heat or cold on my face anymore.

"If you can see me Paul, your baby is being born today," I blurted out through a fake scream.

The ground shook again. All the applause and cheers tailed away. I wanted the ambulance driver to stop again, to deliver the baby then and there, with the door open and a camera broadcasting the entire act to New York City.

"I think it's time," I said.

"No, hold on. We're almost there," Timothy said, pleading with me, his brow crossed. He read my lie expertly. The paramedic checked me nonetheless.

"You haven't fully dilated yet," he said to the camera with a confused look.

"Why is there so much pain, then?" A resounding awe warmed the area around the ambulance.

We turned down a side street. I couldn't hear my audience anymore, but I had faith they watched me on the big screen overlooking Times Square.

"You have to find a way to reach my husband," I said.

"He is watching somewhere, I'm sure."

"The baby. The baby needs to see him. I don't want a fatherless baby."

"Don't worry, Mrs. Shell. We're praying for you. And we're praying for your husband," he said, as if following a script.

When we reached the hospital, Timothy repositioned the cameraman so that he could get an action shot of the race to the birth scene. As they rolled me out and helped me into a wheelchair, Timothy whispered into the stranger's ear. I wondered why the ambulance had delivered us to a private clinic and not a hospital. My obstetrician was not here, I was sure.

"Timothy?" I whispered under my breath so that my voice wouldn't be picked up by the microphone on the camera.

"Yes, Carol," he whispered back.

"Where are we?"

"Don't worry. We needed somewhere more private to stage the birth scene, something more historic, more humble. Trust me, these doctors are the best money could buy."

He nodded to the cameraman for a close-up as he pushed me into the tiny clinic and down a narrow hallway. When we reached the dimly lit delivery room, Timothy gave the cameraman the cutthroat signal. The room went black. He had other plans.

CHAPTER 27: LEA

I PUT MY FINGER THROUGH THE HOLE in my hand. Paul watched me from the fetal position, comparing wounds.

"I smell roses. Do you smell roses?" he asked me.

"Yes. I smell roses."

I examined my new wounds like they were gifts imparted to me. When I felt the inside flesh of the wounds, a scent of roses emanated. I had read about it somewhere. Roses of the stigmata. Some saints had bled from holes in their hands, feet, and side. Some bled from the temples of their foreheads. All had one commonality: The blood from each wound carried the scent of roses.

Paul moved closer to me. I didn't flinch when he pulled my hand to his nose and sniffed it. "Lea? Your blood. It smells like roses."

I didn't answer him.

"Smell mine."

He tore the wrap and placed his blackening hand to my nose. It smelled foul, infected.

This time, I flinched.

"It hurts more than ever," he said.

I placed my hand in front of my face. I could see Paul through the hole in my palm. It was perfectly hollowed open, like it was carved and smoothed by a carpenter with a plane.

"I didn't hear the drill," he said, thinking out loud.

I refused to answer him. There had been no drill this time

around. These wounds had formed on their own after my vision. I had finally found the reason for my stories.

"Your head is bleeding too," he observed.

I wiped a stream of blood there. The blood was clean, thin, and bright.

"What did they do to your head and your side? Your side is bleeding through the cloth."

I hadn't felt the bleeding at my side yet. I was too captivated by the holes in my hands and feet, their perfectly circular design. They didn't bleed to cover the holes. The blood didn't collect in the void. It simply flowed down my arms or into the spaces between my toes.

Paul put his finger through the hole in my foot. "How did they make it so perfect?" he asked.

"I don't know."

"Why didn't I hear the drill? Why didn't you wake me to watch?"

"I tried waking you. I thought you were dead."

"I smell like I'm dying. I feel my wounds turning another colour. It feels green, especially this hand." He showed me his right. A darkened rash had spread to his wrist. I finally paid him attention, although I had no words of consolation to offer him.

"Do you care about the story anymore? Or just the poem?" he asked.

"What story?"

"The story we were going to tell about our army, our country, our leaders. How they've been killing Western journalists in Iraq to strike fear in our voices, to alter the medium of propaganda."

"Do you really care about our country anymore, Paul? Do you think words like *justice* have any meaning here or there?" I laughed. "I care more for the poem."

"What about the story? The people back home need to know. We have suffered enough to tell it. We have to tell it now. Otherwise, what purpose has there been?"

"It is its own purpose."

"Next time they film us, we'll scream it out. We'll scream the truth. Everyone will hear us. They will know we are true in our suffering."

"We'll destroy their innocence, Paul. It's all they have."

"But we'll expose these bastards for what they are."

"Which is?"

He was silent. He didn't know yet. I answered for him.

"Exactly what they claim to be. Artists of torture."

I got up and walked to the door. I leaned my ear on it and heard nothing. They would surely return. If we managed to tell our story, it might destroy the marriage. I had always believed in the contraries. Hell needed a Heaven to corrupt, and Heaven needed an enemy to destroy. Could one story do anything but state what everyone already knew? The two needed each other to exist. Without the marriage, there would be no stories worth remembering. There would be nothing to create.

"My hand is hurting. Please soothe it," he begged me. I read his true intentions. He wanted to smell roses one more time. I knocked on the door instead.

"What are you doing?"

"Inviting them in."

CHAPTER 28: CAROL

M Y BABY WAS BORN IN DARKNESS, in the soft light of a single candle. Timothy paid the doctors to reserve the darkest room on the delivery floor, furthest away from the possibility of any artificial, exposed light. He might have even grown paranoid of the sun. He ordered blinds for the windows. The men who installed them taped them tight to the panes. I half-slept through my contractions. I hadn't felt any since the tanned man entered the room to stick a long needle into my spine. Paralysis would give him more time, Timothy decided, to get the room ready, to have it entirely blocked from light, to have security police guarding the door and a helicopter outside fending off other helicopters desperate to get the first picture.

"Why do you want the baby to be born in the dark?" the doctor asked him, while I listened, feigning sleep.

"I don't trust your nurses or you. We need the first pictures of this baby. This baby is a special baby. Everyone will want a picture of this baby."

"You're going to sell the baby's picture?"

Timothy raised his phone to his ear, holding a finger to motion for silence while he murmured assent to an unheard voice. He put the phone back down.

"I've already had bids."

"You're selling the baby before it is born?" The doctor said this in my direction.

Timothy answered for me. "Are you judging us, doctor?"

The doctor remained quiet. He was young, with a military symbol on his palm—a green demon with a rifle, just like Timothy's.

"Do you have a husband kidnapped by terrorists? Are you alone? Do you have a new baby that will depend on you and you alone for the rest of his or her life?" Timothy said, like a well-practiced preacher.

The doctor glanced at me, his face softening, the judgment therein dissipating with watery eyes.

"Then you do the job you have been paid for, doctor, and let me do mine."

The phone vibrated. Timothy took the call.

"Yes, almost there. Your price is going to have to be higher. The pictures will be perfect. I have a photographer arriving any minute to get the first shot. The best shooter I know."

The doctor bumped into a standing monitor. He mumbled something to himself, hissing the words. Timothy walked in circles again. I followed the blue light from his phone.

"This is Paul Shell's only child. Six hundred thousand is the starting point."

The doctor separated my legs. I couldn't feel them. They floated above me on the wings of my feet. Frustrated, he left the room. He returned a short time later with a hard hat. He must have stolen it from a construction worker outside. A light shone from the top, blanking his face.

"Hold on there doctor, the photographer hasn't arrived yet," Timothy said, placing him on pause.

"I'm just checking her dilation. She's isn't close to ready yet."

"Perfect. Just relax it a little, doc. That's all I'm asking. Give her another needle."

A man burst into the room, pulling a camera from a bag.

"What took you so long?" Timothy asked as if to reprimand him.

"Your police escorts ran a check on me before they let me up."

"Okay, Carol. The examination might induce labour, just

to warn you," the doctor proceeded, stretching gloves over his hands.

I couldn't see the photographer's face. He pulled a cord with a tester from the camera and extended it under the sheet. The doctor glanced over his shoulder, before returning his attention to me.

"Okay Carol, are you ready?"

"I can't feel anything."

"Nurse, can you prepare the vacuum and forceps just in case we need them later?" He waved a shiny, gloved hand to the nurse.

"Hold on, hold on," interrupted Timothy.

"What is it now?"

"I just thought of something. Can we get a Caesarean?"

"Excuse me?"

"A Caesarean section. I was just thinking. We want that baby clean for a good picture. We don't want its head to be egg-shaped or oval. That baby's got to be beautiful, as soon as it comes out."

"I can't do that."

The doctor rose to remove his latex gloves, clean from not having entered me yet. I worried as he threatened to leave the room.

"What are you doing, doctor?" Timothy said, raising his voice.

"I am not delivering this baby. Not like this."

"What is wrong with you doctors? You have the vanity to speak of yourselves as the only wise ones around."

"What are you talking about?"

"You will deliver this baby via Caesarean."

The doctor opened himself up to me for a second opinion. I experienced the whole scene, but the drugs had softened the impact of the conflict before me. I thought they were simply planning the event of my baby's birth or discussing names. I read somewhere, in one of my baby preparation manuals, that in the past, midwives would assign names to the babies they delivered. Would my doctor do the same?

"You want me to cut her open in this darkness," he said, the argument ensuing.

"Precisely. That's how they used to do it, right?"

"How do you expect I do that?"

"Come on, doctor. I'm sure you've done enough of these for a lifetime. It will be like holding a candle in the sunshine."

Timothy pressed an envelope against the doctor's lab coat. The doctor asked the nurse to hold the candle near him so he could see where he was cutting. The photographer pulled up a chair to stand on it for a bird's-eye view. He hovered above me in the dark, like a spider dangling on an electrical wire.

The doctor proceeded with the surgery. I didn't feel anything. I didn't have to push. They gave me more morphine, but I fought it to stay awake. Before long, I saw a baby rise from the stained sheets in the flickering of a candle held in the palm of the nurse's hand. Flashes of the flame made my newborn move, cry in slow motion. Timothy held my hand tight like a husband. I felt Paul in the room again. He might have died already, I feared. Perhaps he would attend his daughter's birth in spirit. They placed the bloody baby on my chest. It wriggled around in the stained towel. I could hear Timothy's voice.

"Clean it off. Clean it off."

The photographer continued to shoot from all angles, so fast that the snapping sound overlapped onto itself in the tiled room.

The nurse put the candle aside to clean the baby. My daughter's head was round and her eyes creased. Timothy started the applause. The others reluctantly joined him.

"What is her name?" the nurse asked.

"We want to call her Pauline, after her father," Timothy said.

"Mary," I murmured from my drug daze, but no one listened enough to consider it.

THEY TOOK MY BABY AWAY FROM ME for a long time. I waited in the dark delivery room where they left me to sleep in the dark. More and more, I felt the tearing pain from the incision. I needed painkillers. I wanted to see my daughter. I waited for the door to open.

Timothy entered a short time later with an ambivalent face. I couldn't read it properly.

"What is it, Timothy?"

"I have good news and bad news. Which do you want to hear first, Carol?"

"The bad news."

"The bad news is you are no longer the number one search on the Internet."

My stomach dropped as swiftly as when the baby had been carved out, leaving an empty hole. It deflated inwards.

"What do you mean, Timothy?"

"Your daughter has usurped your position."

Timothy extended his arms out to announce the surprise, while I crossed my arms.

"What is the good news, Timothy?"

"You earned a hefty prize for your nine months of sacrifice."

"You sold them already."

"Before they cleaned her ears out."

"What was the price?"

"More than thirty silver pieces, that's for sure," he said, laughing. I wasn't amused this time by his sarcasm.

"I do have a tiebreaker, though."

"What is that?"

"A spot on the *New Living Show*. Just in time for the release of your book. You and Pauline."

"Both of us?"

"Yes. She wanted the both of you. All we need now is for him to die and make you a widow."

"A widowed baby," I whispered to myself, but he heard it with his sonic ears.

"That's just perfect. A widowed baby. We can sell that in a heartbeat."

CHAPTER 29: **LEA**

WE HAD NEVER INVITED the torturers to the torture room before, although they arrived as if invited, carrying the gift of weapons with them. They arrived on the echo of my knock.

"What are you doing?" Paul asked me before they entered.

"I'm calling them."

"Why?"

"I want them to torture us."

"You haven't had enough?"

"We are getting stronger while they are getting weaker."

"I am not getting stronger."

The door broke open. Instinctively, I ran away from it, afraid. Paul shimmied to the wall to avoid the light.

A taller man entered. His footsteps slapped the pavement with authority. He didn't say anything. He sniffed aloud over and over again. He inhaled one long breath, and then he watched both of us for a few seconds in silence. Others followed him in, repeating the sniffing. His voice gave orders without wavering. The men behind him hesitated before they obeyed. I placed my bleeding hands under my arms to hide their scent, but the man had seen them already.

He walked over to me. In an angry voice, he called others over to inspect them. They spoke with speed, competing in a race for the right answer, each voice hurrying to catch up to the other. Two men pulled me up. One grabbed my bleeding side. He placed his hand to his nose. The other fingered my bleeding feet. All at once, they turned their attention to Paul as if to blame him.

"Why are they looking at me that way?" Paul asked me.

"They think you did this to me."

"Why would they think that?"

"Because they didn't do this to me."

Paul rose to his feet.

The leader made an order in a loud voice. A group of men entered to counter the threat. They approached him with small steps, provoking him to sink to the ground again, covering his face. One man grabbed his gangrenous hand, and as if pressing the pain button, Paul screamed. The man sniffed the infected hand. He spat on the floor, disgusted. He yelled for a solution. Another man came in with tools and the chair.

"No, not the chair. Please, not the chair."

Paul tried to slide out of their grips. They dragged him by his feet to the chair. A man with a tool belt removed a stone, and I heard him scratching it with a butcher's knife, before wiping the blade on the belt. Paul begged for them to punish me instead. "Do it to her. Do it to her. You did it to me already."

A blunt strike to his mouth cut off his speech. Paul began to cry, the silky tears blending with the flow of blood and teeth that trickled from his mouth and down onto his naked chest.

The scarf with the tool belt pulled Paul's hands through tight, leather straps. Another man held Paul's head back by the chin, pressing his jaw shut.

The man with the tool belt walked around Paul, screaming in his face. He spat on the ground. He spat in Paul's face. He spat on the smelly hand. The others joined him in his tribal chant.

As the sounds culminated to a screaming pitch, the young boy in the scarf stood in the middle of them with his hands up.

"He didn't do it. He didn't do it. I did it."

Everyone in the room stopped. He looked at me, and I could tell he was lying.

The man with the tool belt wasn't convinced. He screamed at the boy in their native tongue, shaking his finger before dismissing him from the room. He revved up the others again with the same repeated phrase and a stamp of his foot. Before long, the sounds had reached a chorus and eventually a tribal cry.

Suddenly separating himself from the group, the leader of the chant removed the butcher knife from his belt and cut Paul's hand at the wrist in a single motion. Paul lost consciousness immediately, before his hand had time to flop to the cement. As if knowing their clean-up roles, a man with a white towel recovered it from the room while a shorter man unstrapped Paul from the chair. Once they cleared the debris, the tallest one in the group slung Paul's body over his shoulder like a sack of bones. The big man who first entered the room unlocked the two doors on the same wall. As the doors opened, I saw closets holding trash, old rags, and broken tools. More dead ends.

The taller man slid Paul up against the door while another bent his arms, backwards over the top of the door. He tied his wrists together with rope and tightened it on the other side of the door by stretching his arms with the leverage provided by the top of the door. He pulled on it until Paul's ribs stretched and cracked. The sound woke him suddenly. He couldn't breathe. He was barely able to see from the loss of blood. The man tightened a knot on the door handle.

They hung me on the door facing him in the same way. Before they left the room, two or three of them inspected my wounds again, nodding, humming, and hyperventilating in-between words in a kind of sexual ecstasy. The door to the room closed a short time later.

"I'm going to stop breathing," Paul said, choking on his words.

"You can't."

"I can't breathe."

"Me neither."

"We are going to die."

"We will not die this way."

"Why not?"

"It doesn't serve their purpose."

"They cut my hand off."

"It smelled. It would have killed you before they were ready."

Paul stopped talking. He agreed with me.

"They didn't film us this time," he said.

"They have something else in mind."

"What is that?"

"They are trying to immortalize themselves. They want to create something."

Paul's breathing became wet in the air. I could feel his spit against my face. "Did he really do that to you? The boy?"

"No, he lied."

"Why would he lie?"

"To spare himself or to save us."

Paul paused for a moment. "If they kill me," he said, his thoughts taking on a new direction, "I want you to watch me die. Don't turn away. I want you to see me die."

"Why is that?"

"I want you to save me."

"How can I save you?"

"When you go home, I want you to remember how I died. Someone will ask you for the story."

"What makes you so sure they will kill you first?"

"They will fear killing you. You are too beautiful in your suffering. They recognize the stigmata, the symbol of saintliness from another religion. "

"They have killed many others, I'm sure."

"They didn't bleed roses. You bleed roses."

I could feel my wounds softening before a new release of blood flowed from my body. Paul stared at my face. A stream of blood soaked into my eyelashes from a mysterious wound on my forehead. I did not feel weak.

"I'll ask them to kill me for you," I said.

"No, you won't. You won't steal my death from me."

"But your wife. Your child."

"While we hung from the chains, I dreamt about the birth. The baby was a boy. He looked like my father when he was young. Curly hair. Blue eyes."

"I have a daughter," I confessed directly.

"All this time, and you never told me."

"She died inside of me, and I had to give birth to a dead baby. Stillborn. The story of her life. Born still. But I never realized, until now, that she is alive. She didn't die. We will never die."

"Do you think you will ever see her again?"

"Yes. Without the stillness."

"My son will never remember me," Paul said with acceptance.

"But he will make up stories to believe in you. You will be heroic in those stories. And he will discover you in his life. He will feel you in his movements. He will see you as a man he never wants to be, only dream about."

Paul smiled at me. It pleased him.

"If they kill me, I will scream their injustices before they do so."

"The world will hear you if you do, and it will not care, Paul. The world prefers to forget its history now, like an ignored conscience."

"Let it hear me anyway. I will have my say."

The scarves re-entered the room with cameras, but the young boy wasn't among them this time. The man with the tool belt entered last, behind the huddle. Another scarf held a different camera. This camera was newer, and I caught flashes of silver as they twisted it onto a tripod. It was wired to the laptop being wheeled into the room. I whispered over to Paul.

"Do you see him?"

"Who?"

"The boy."

"No."

"They're filming us live."

"A podcast?" he whispered back.

"Yes."

The camera scanned our bodies from top to bottom slowly, as if to size them up for dissection. One man narrated in broken English.

"As you can see, we have hurt them bad. We did not ask for much. But you gave us nothing. We have no choice now."

The man who had scooped up Paul's hand unwrapped it from the towel. The camera zoomed in on the green hand with the hole in the palm. They had created their own special effect.

The man holding the light shined it at Paul to strengthen the association, while the camera avoided a close-up of my new wounds. Another hooded man cut Paul down and he crashed, knees first, onto the cement. I watched him from my position above. He looked up to me. I could read what he was about to say before he said it. He waited for them to pull him up from the ground so he could stick his face to the camera, like a true television journalist.

"You are killing your own journalists here. You want to save the marriage of war, of Good and Evil, by silencing our voices. Our stories expose the hypocrisy of war. So, you've made a pact with the Devil and married your interests to terrorists in order to keep war alive and profitable. You want to avoid the divorce of peace, so you continue to wage war against your own truth-bearers. They are killing us because you asked them to."

The man with the tool belt quickly pulled a curved sword from over his shoulder while the others pressed the neck down. Paul's head rolled to the floor with a paralyzed smile.

CHAPTER 30: LEA

AFTER THEY REMOVED PAUL'S BODY from the room, the light-skinned Dragon Man entered, his face adorned flamboyantly with a red scarf. I hung from the door, my arms tied at the wrists to the doorknob on the other side. He looked up to me and in his grey eyes I saw devotion and uncertainty. He spoke in choppy, military English, with a southern twang. "Where did you get those wounds?"

"I don't know."

"We will kill you if you do not tell us."

"I cannot tell you because I do not know."

As he interrogated me, the others brought in a long bench. They adjusted its angle and loosened the straps. Their rusted steel buckles clanged to the floor.

"Did you cut those yourself?"

"No. I have nothing to cut myself with."

He walked up to me and sniffed, but my scent didn't annoy him. His eyes closed to enjoy it. "We will clean your mind."

They cut me down from the door, and when I hit the cement bottom, the air in the room nearly drowned me in one swallow. I heaved on the ground where Paul's head had spilled.

Someone from behind me wrapped my face with a thin cloth. I could breathe through the veil, almost see through it. They pulled me to the bench by the elbows, refusing to touch the parts of my body that bled, as if they contained an infectious disease that could cure them of their ways.

They laid me down on the bench and strapped me to it, my feet elevated above me but not quite upside down. I could feel blood falling to my brain. My head felt heavy with it.

I heard the hose being pulled in again and stretched out to avoid the impediment of knots. Water travelled through the pipe and exploded onto my face.

I sunk into an ocean of cerulean blue, and I couldn't swim to the surface. My legs felt too heavy and my arms not strong enough against the undertow.

I gagged out loud, spitting water upwards against the flow. I couldn't catch up to it before it entered my lungs. I had reported on waterboarding once before. In every account, it was described as the ultimate tool of torture. To think, that water could pose such a threat when you were always thirsty.

I thought I would die inside myself first. My spirit was drowning inside the watery tomb of this leftover body. I would definitely drown within myself. Then it stopped.

"Who gave you those wounds? The boy?"

I couldn't speak. I coughed water and unintelligible sounds. "A saint," I finally said.

"What saint? There are no saints here."

"The one in the brown robe."

Silence.

Water slapped my face again with the force of an open hand. It travelled up my nose, flooding my ears, and pushed my tongue backwards into my throat.

I tried to think of something that would distract me from the belief I would drown, but the only memories that surfaced were those of when I was a tiny girl in a yellow church dress playing outside my grandfather's home on Pine Street. The angels in his apricot tree called me to climb up. I was afraid of them then. I hid in his dirty shed, waiting for them to go away because I didn't want to join them after my grandfather died. I was waiting for him to return and take me with him by hand. He was always my guardian after my father died. He spoke to me, saying, "The worship of God is: Honouring his gifts in other men each according to his genius.'"

At the time, I didn't understand him. He spoke in riddles and opposites. Although I didn't understand them, I had come to appreciate the opposing natures of belief. I had accepted them. I had assumed them without knowing.

The man was squeezing the hose for I could still feel some water sprinkling on my face. "I am going to ask you again. Where did you get those wounds?"

I gagged up water again. My lungs felt full of it, in need of desert air to dry them up, and yet, I was dry in my mouth, almost chafed, thirsty. "You."

"We didn't do this to you."

"I made them for you."

I could hear conversation. With Paul gone, the room grew larger in my perception. Doors opened and a window even formed in my imagination. Paul had broken through the cement with his sacrifice. He had shown me the invaluable lesson of letting go. They wouldn't be able to mortar the holes he carved out for me in the room. He had punched them open for me, so that I could see beyond their darkness, so that I could see beyond the walls I had erected in myself. He had saved me in so many ways. They had killed him, but his joy had escaped.

The men exited the room, leaving me strapped to the bench. The water flow decreased. All that was left was a drip on my forehead, repeating itself over and over again.

CHAPTER 31: CAROL

I SAT IN FRONT OF THE MIRROR, alone, surrounded by flowers. After Paul's spectacle of a funeral, I had grown accustomed to being surrounded by them, so I requested them wherever I went. Not just one bouquet. I desired the effort and expertise of floral arrangements. To be surrounded by provisions for my happiness.

A young intern entered the room of flowers. "Mrs. Shell. I will come and retrieve you in five minutes."

Timothy entered the room next, pushing the flowers aside as he carved his way to me. "Pauline is in her dressing room with the nanny, ready when you are."

He spoke to my reflection in the mirror. "Your face is porcelain, Carol."

"Dr. D. is a magician."

"This is what we've prepared ourselves for, honey. We couldn't have orchestrated it better."

"Are we still virtuous?" I asked.

"Excuse me?"

"What we've done. Are we virtuous in our intentions?"

"Of course. There is a baby in the next room who will be taken care of for the rest of her life."

"Which sacrifice is greater?" I asked his reflection in the mirror again.

"What do you mean?"

"His or mine?"

Timothy turned around. He dipped his head into a bouquet to smell it. "I love the scent of roses. I don't know why. It's like it comes from the thorns instead of the flower."

"You're not answering my question, Timothy."

"You can't measure your virtue to anyone else's. No virtue can exist without breaking the Ten Commandments. Even Jesus Christ acted from impulse, not from rules. Creation is its own rule."

I felt at ease again. Timothy could always convince me not to take myself so seriously. I preferred to exist in the utopian landscapes he created for me. Blue skies and fields of flowers. No reasons to worry. He swallowed worries whole and spit out the seeds, as if to fertilize my dreams. He didn't need to reinvent anything for me if he could steal it just the same. My husband could have used him more efficiently, like I had. Paul didn't have to go to war to have his head cut off on the Internet. He could have offered it to Timothy in New York where it would have been bronzed for everyone to admire. If only Paul would have trusted in homegrown stories, like I had.

"Are you ready, Carol? Olivia Manna is the best interview in the world. Your name will burn in lights and cool in gold."

I stood up straight, flattened my belly with a hand, turned around, and received his long, sharp tongue in my mouth.

The intern entered the room to guide me through hallways lined with signed pictures of every celebrity I had ever envied.

Another headset intern spoke directions as we walked. "Olivia wants you to carry the baby in with you. Our live audience will love it."

We stopped at the next dressing room, the one positioned closer to the stage. The nanny, whose name I had forgotten, raised Pauline from the bassinet. I stretched out my arms, but my daughter struggled violently to disentangle herself. I tried to hold her, but she wouldn't accept the firmness of my newly enhanced chest.

"What's wrong with her?" I demanded of the nanny.

"I don't know. Ever since the needle yesterday, she has been feverish."

"The needle?" I asked Timothy, who stood behind me.

"Immunizations. To protect her," he explained.

I tried to rock her. I tried to settle her before we walked on stage. I held her head in my palm to protect it from the violent movements, to support the neck that couldn't hold it up yet.

The intern was impatient.

"Can we get the baby some Tylenol? Something to knock her out," he suggested.

I looked up to Timothy for guidance.

"Sure, put her to sleep, she will appear more innocent that way, " he answered for me.

CHAPTER 32: **LEA**

I COUNTED MEMORIES IN-BETWEEN EACH DROP. It was a game I devised to distract my attention from each tiny dollop of water splashing on the same spot of my forehead.

The day I found a plastic doll in the grass. I was a young girl. The doll had curly blonde hair, which I envied. I wanted curly blonde hair. I kidnapped her from the dandelion field where I had been lying by myself, and back at the house, I dressed her and named her, "Carly." I combed her blonde hair, slept beside her, threw tea parties. I had forgotten what happened to that doll. I remembered moving and never seeing it again. Perhaps I had abandoned it.

A drop on my forehead.

My wedding dance. The song was so sad. Every time I circled around on the empty dance floor, I saw ugly happy faces. They killed me with smiles. I wanted to cry while the wedding photographer tried to get a good shot. He interrupted the dance and pulled us apart on the dance floor. Our feet stopped moving to the music as we posed for a picture, and I sunk my head on his shoulder. I didn't want the song to end. I wanted to dance endlessly in his arms. The very thought of it ending made me despair in white.

A drop on my forehead.

The first day I met Joel. He was a young photographer who showed me needles and drugs to take away the pain. When I didn't notice, in one of my hallucinogenic dreams, he slipped himself inside of me, like a needle in a vein. He told me he didn't believe in love: "There are too many worlds in opposition, colliding, for love to exist."

He showed me how to take pictures because he said he was going to die one day. He told me to believe in the still image. It was truth to him. No one could change it, only burn it. I could exchange this truth to those who needed something to rely on, something to look at. I watched him collapse in the middle of the street. He had left his good camera and the better lenses in the red room for me, as if he had known. He had purchased enough film to document a lifetime. I hid it.

A drop on my forehead.

The day the pox-faced man tapped me on the shoulder in church. My mother had sent me to confession. After telling the priest the same lies as always, I kneeled before the statue of a bearded man with a heart belted by thorns. I prayed for him not to talk to me anymore. I was sick of his voice. I didn't want to follow. I didn't want to have a heart like his. I didn't want to have anything that red and vulnerable. On his painted hands, I saw delicate slivers of blood. His feet were beautifully manicured in the same colour. Flesh and blood. He was too beautiful to be broken, I remembered thinking. Too in love with me to let me go. And then the man who prayed the Stations of the Cross tapped me on the shoulder. My mother had warned me of him.

"Stay away from him. He is a crazy man."

He scared me, and I ran away.

I hurried this memory, expecting another drop of water to interrupt it. But the drop scattered in mid-air instead, sprinkling my entire face. The fault line of a distant explosion rocked the room, quaking the ground, lifting it, and arching my back in the process. The straps tightened against my limbs. Another thumping followed after a siren-like call from the sky warned of its heavy landing. I couldn't see anything with the damp veil sticking to my face, but I could hear gunfire. And I could easily imagine the art of war at work. The insurrection of colourful earth dotted with streaks of bullets as they sliced the dust into straight lines. Windows shattering. Wooden tables splintering. Fruit bouncing to cold ceramic floors and rolling away to resistant walls. Church bells ringing in the distance, souls rising, bodies falling, imprints of sneakers marking the sand. Children running for hiding spots, mothers praying within screams, breasts leaking milk for babies needing to latch. Backs of legs mapping varicose veins. Clothes on a frantic line swaying between buildings. The safety of routine invaded by men in boots, gun carriage visitations, grenade clicks. Small talk interrupted by panicked imploring. *"Where is she? Where is he? Another one is coming."*

The sound of boots became louder upon approach and the gunshots more subtle, not so rhythmic. Was I being rescued? Were people dying in order to free me from this purgatory of water? Had my captors resolved to protect the woman who bled roses from her wounds?

I waited. My forehead was drying in the open air. The water line had been cut off. I heard footsteps prattling to the room, then, just as quickly, departing past. They were outside the walls, and I didn't scream to reach them. I didn't want to be found, like in the red room. They passed my room like the desert wind, in fleets. After a while, I could hear the sprinkle of dust settling on the roof. No saviour, just the readjustment of matter in the crevices and holes and stone.

In that moment, I understood that war didn't happen on the outside, as much as it was born from the inside. The battles were simply manifestations of thoughts, feelings, hurt, love, hatred, pain. They were imagined as I imagined them, from the deepest cores of fear, from the perils of nothing.

In the prolonged silence of expectation, a buzzing became louder as it penetrated the cracks in the building. It was a soft buzzing, like a bee's in search of pollen. A hovering sound almost sexually exhaustive in the aftermath of this recent attack, in the clearing of combat. It carried a blossoming scent of gasoline.

A kickstand clicked, and the buzzing disappeared. Before long, an asthmatic breathing entered the room. Who was this loosening me from the straps? My body convulsed upon the release, epileptic. The broken pieces flowed together into the liquid of my body. I felt clean. Baptized.

Hands pulled me to the sitting position, a man's strength in a boy's fingertips. Was he going to release all that I had absorbed now or let me die in peace? He lifted the veil as my husband once did, slowly.

I saw a young man's face. It was beautiful, angelic to the sight. I had never seen a face so remarkably porcelain. Clean of blemishes. Tanned with dark eyebrows and lashes that I recognized from another lifetime. His was the only name that came to mind. I had photographed those eyes once.

"Adnan?"

He nodded, smiled. When the light around his head filtered away, I saw the room where I had been kept. Sunlight revealed it to me. The torture room had been a bedroom once before. A place where someone slept, dressed, staged dreams. The two doors where Paul and I once hung were insignificant doors that kept dust away from clothes or white shirts. The floor was tiled with linoleum. There were nails in the wall that once held portraits. Someone lived here before we suffered and died here. I could feel the residue of memories sticking to the walls.

"Where am I?"

"You are in a room."

"How did you find me?"

"I was called by a sign."

"You were called by a sign?"

"I saw my name on television, on the wall."

He got up and walked to the plastered wall where Paul preferred to sleep. Adnan's name was scratched in the wall in a young boy's big handwriting.

"I have been here before. I mean, I lived here before," he said.

He offered me his hand. When I took it, I realized there wasn't a hole in mine anymore. I checked the other hand, then my head, and finally my side. No wounds. No bleeding. For some reason, I felt sad.

"What is it?"

"Nothing. I used to bleed."

"I know. It's a good thing we are filled with blood."

I walked out of the abandoned basement with the ease of having owned the place, like a home. When we exited the room, I observed the area on the other side of the door. The weapons used to create our torture hung like trophies from the walls. On the floor, lay a body covered with a blanket. On top of the blanket rested a book. I picked it up. It was the book of the sketch artist. Each of the pages depicted a different torture. A sketched history. A piece of authentic art.

"Leave it be," Adnan said, as he tried to edge me out of the room.

"I want to see," I said, pointing to the blanket, assuming it was Paul's body they had left behind.

Adnan obeyed and lowered the edge of the sheet like he did my veil, slowly.

It was the boy behind the computer, without a scarf. His eyelids were closed. His beautiful, long eyelashes remained, still curled. Instead of crying, I felt the urge to swaddle him for some reason, make him believe he was still in his mother's womb so that he could sleep more soundly, be more trusting of an uninviting world, but he was at peace under the blanket, so I simply covered him up again.

ON HIS VESPA, ADNAN DROVE ME through the desert, and the landscape transformed from how I remembered it.

"Where did those mountains come from?" I asked.

"The hand of God, I assume," he said, laughing. "Or your imagination."

In the front basket, a paper bag crackled in the wind. I feared there was a bottle in it for me.

"Where are you taking me?"

"I am taking you where it is green and safe."

I stared at the mountain line. It formed a wall against the sky that I imagined myself climbing over.

"Stop."

"We are in the middle of the desert, Lea."

"Please, stop. I need to find something."

"What could you possibly find in a flat desert?"

He had not seen the mountains of sand, "Hills like white elephants," as Hemingway once wrote.

"My story. It's time to find my story on the other side."

He stopped the Vespa in the middle of the road. Civilization seemed further away in time, the mountains closer to my bare feet.

"Thank you."

He looked at me like the mother who once told him his father died. I pressed my footsteps into the sand on my way to the mountainside. Behind me, I could hear the Vespa buzzing away and then the screech of brakes. It looped around and stopped on skidded rubber.

"Lea?"

Adnan leaned the Vespa onto its kickstand. He walked over to deliver the paper bag.

"Your things. I took them from the red room."

I received them from him as a parting gift and nodded as I once did to dismiss him from the red room, when I couldn't bear to look at him, when I felt so ashamed to look at him. Now I realized he was better off leaving me, and I was better off letting him go.

He had one more question to ask me. I could detect confusion in his young and shiny face. "What are 'chinks?'"

I smiled. "Openings to understanding."

He nodded as if to finally understand something as an adult

would. Satisfied, he left me alone with my things. The buzzing and the cloud of dust trailing the Vespa dissipated into the heat.

I sat in the sand, depositing the contents of the paper bag before me. My laptop. My prayer book with the needle encased as a bookmark. Some clothes. A full bottle of grain alcohol with symbols on the label. Joel's camera. Adnan had found the hiding place.

I stared at the collection in the sand and reached for the prayer book with the needle. I had inherited it from my grandfather, the prayer book that is. The smell of the leather reminded me of the old smell of his bristled face against mine. When I broke the elastic band, I realized this book was not the same prayer book from the red room, nor was it the one my torturers had left us in the dark room.

The pages had blanked. Clean cream pages. No words or scripture. No proverbs or poems. No story in-between the lines.

The needle had fallen into the sand. When I retrieved my makeshift bookmark, I realized the point had changed as well. Not a needle point, but a pen point. It was steel and sharpened like a quill.

I rose to my feet with both in hand and walked away from the debris of a former life. The mountains, whether they existed or not, invited me to climb in the historic distance. If I managed to reach the top, I knew I would find the right ending, the one to congeal everything and prevent my story from falling apart, drifting away, or settling into nothing. With blank pages and the poison of ink, as Paul would say, I could create a new story out of Hell, out of nothing.

The desert brightness surrounded me with warmth and yellow sand. The memory of palm trees behind me in the city. A sky without clouds or the threat of rain. A terrestrial void, which called itself to be filled by a prophetic voice.

I felt like singing. Random verses from a poem I once made into a song to soften my daughter's relentless kicking, when she was alive, when she was inside me and safe.

ACKNOWLEDGEMENTS

I would like to take this opportunity to acknowledge poems like William Blake's "The Marriage of Heaven and Hell" for further inspiring my obsession with religious text, and for validating my passion for mystical narratives. As a child, these stories seemed to find me, and strengthen my desire for prayer. From these humble, spiritual beginnings, I never thought these influences would have such a profound effect on my style as a writer. I sincerely consider myself gifted by their wisdom.

In this same faithful light, I would like to thank Luciana Ricciutelli, Editor-in-Chief at Inanna Publications, for her belief in this work. Also, I would like to acknowledge the editors who sharpened its construction, and offered exceptional suggestions for its improvement.

I consider myself privileged to be part of an extended and supportive family that takes pride in the aspirations of its relatives. More specifically, I would like to thank my mother, Marcella, for her beautiful devotion and love, my brothers, Frank and Ryan, for the motivating example they set, and my father, Leonardo, who unfortunately passed this year. He was a man who shone with the brightness of a star and the heart of a saint. His words, still alive in my thoughts, and although often broken by English, are the power behind everything I write. All of my work will be forever dedicated to his memory. Finally, I would like to acknowledge my every day inspirations. My beautifully strong and supportive wife, Lauren; my children, Aidan, Oscar, Tobias, and Alaia; and our new dog, Gigi, always find ways to show me the unconditional graces of family love. I pledge every word I write, to all of you. My life's dreams are yours, as is my heart.

Dean Serravalle is the author of the novels *Reliving Charley,* *Lock 7,* and *Chameleon (Days)*, a national award-winning teacher, and the founder of Writers4peace, a non-profit organization which aims to mentor students interested in publishing writing aimed at social justice issues. He lives in Niagara Falls, Ontario.